A BEAR'S BRIDE

A RETELLING OF EAST OF THE SUN, WEST OF THE MOON

SHARI L. TAPSCOTT

ALSO BY SHARI L. TAPSCOTT

Silver & Orchids

Moss Forest Orchid
Greybrow Serpent
Wildwood Larkwing
Lily of the Desert
Fire & Feathers: Novelette Prequel to Moss Forest Orchid

Eldentimber Series

Pippa of Lauramore
Anwen of Primewood
Seirsha of Errinton
Rosie of Triblue
Audette of Brookraven
Elodie of the Sea
Grace of Vernow: An Eldentimber Novelette

Fairy Tale Kingdoms

The Marquise and Her Cat: A Puss in Boots Retelling
The Queen of Gold and Straw: A Rumpelstiltskin Retelling

CONTEMPORARY FICTION

The Glitter and Sparkle Series

Glitter and Sparkle
Shine and Shimmer
Sugar and Spice

If the Summer Lasted Forever
Just the Essentials

A Bear's Bride: A Retelling of East of the Sun, West of the Moon
Entwined Tales - Vol. 3
Copyright © 2018 by Shari L. Tapscott
All rights reserved.
ISBN: 9781723995477

This book or any portion thereof may not be reproduced or used in any manner whatsoever without the express written permission of the publisher except for the use of brief quotations in a book review.

This is a work of fiction. Names, characters, businesses, places, events and incidents are either the products of the author's imagination or used in a fictitious manner. Any resemblance to actual persons, living or dead, or actual events is purely coincidental.

Editing by Z.A. Sunday & Melanie Cellier
Cover Design by Myrrhlynn & Page Nine Media

*For the Indie Bunch ladies
You guys rock.*

ENTWINED TALES

A Goose Girl
K. M. Shea

An Unnatural Beanstalk
Brittany Fichter

A Bear's Bride
Shari L. Tapscott

A Beautiful Curse
Kenley Davidson

A Little Mermaid
Aya Ling

An Inconvenient Princess
Melanie Cellier

MAP

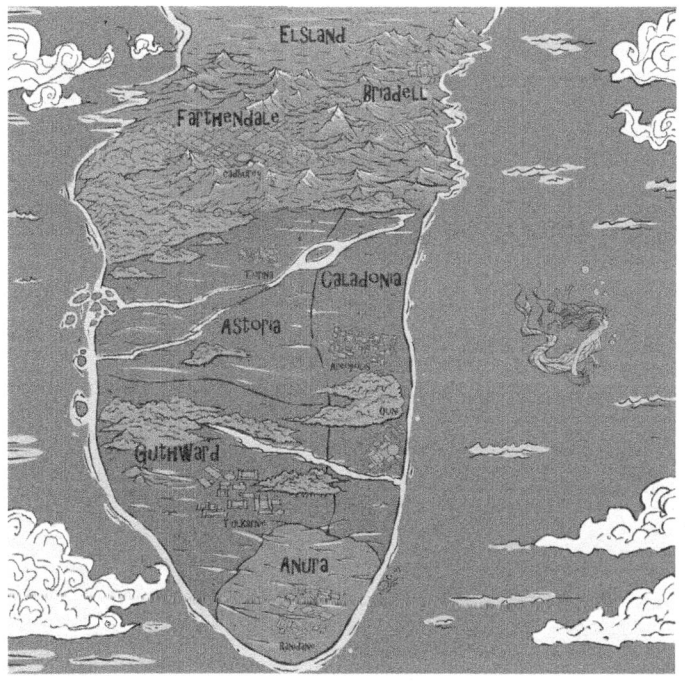

CHAPTER 1

The alley behind the farrier's barn is the perfect location for meetings of the clandestine variety. A weeping willow grows right behind a tool shed, blocking the view of the street, and an old cart with a broken wheel and a busted tongue sits on the other side, creating the perfect cover.

With a quick glance over my shoulder to make sure no one has spotted me, I slip behind the barn.

Peter leans against the wagon. His long, lean body is relaxed, and a lazy smile stretches across his face as soon as he sees me.

There isn't a girl in Torina who doesn't walk by his father's shop several times a week, hoping to catch a glimpse of him. Even Anneliese, my flighty, impulsive younger sister, notices him despite the gap in their ages.

I'm old enough to court the apprentice tailor—but I'm more than happy to let the other girls have him.

"You're late," Peter murmurs as he loops an arm

around my waist, playfully pulling me close and moving in to steal a kiss. "I have to be back soon, or Father will have my head."

I'm never late, not ever. I always arrive exactly when I plan to. Whether that coincides with other people's schedules is another matter entirely.

"Peter, get off," I say, laughing as I shove him away.

We've been friends since the time he and I stole his snooty sister's favorite bonnet and placed it on their family's prize pig. She was livid; it was beautiful.

I was six at the time. Peter must have been eight. I'm eighteen now, so we've been a duo for twelve years…and forbidden from seeing each other for two, going on three.

Father says Peter's a "good-for-nothing" and a "bad influence." *I* say Peter's the only person in this dull city who knows how to keep things interesting.

"When do you have to be back to the shop?" I ask him as soon as he unhands me.

He grimaces, his handsome face contorting in a way that makes me smile. "Soon. Lady Milia has requested a gown for the early summer ball."

"That's in less than a week!"

"She pays well." He shrugs. "How are you? I haven't seen you in days. Do your parents have you on animal duty again?"

I lean against the building and huff out a frustrated breath. "Father is making noise about finding me a husband now that Rynn and Eva are married."

Peter frowns, not liking that at all. "What are you going to do?"

"I have no idea."

He joins me by the barn, and his shoulder rests comfortably next to mine. "Do you want to get married, Sophie?"

His tone is off, not Peter-like at all. I turn my head and find him staring at me with the strangest look on his face. "Yes, I suppose. But not to anyone Father chooses."

Shoving a shoulder against the splintering boards, Peter shifts to stand in front of me. He rests a hand on the barn next to my head and leans toward me in a way he's never done before.

I watch him, startled and frankly, a little disconcerted. We've played before, but he's never looked at me like this.

"Marry me," he says, his eyes searching mine.

"*Peter,*" I try to nudge him away like I think he's playing again—though I know very well he's not.

He grins, finding amusement in my discomfort. "I mean it. Let's get married. We'll run away from this dull city, find adventure together. Picture it, Sophie." He holds up his hand in a dramatic fashion. "The two of us, slaying trolls in Elsland, perhaps searching for mermaids off the coast of Caladonia."

I gulp, unsure how to answer. The adventure part sounds lovely…but there's one problem. Peter's only an *apprentice* tailor, and I have no skills to speak of. How would we make a living? I'm afraid I'm used to a comfortable life, and anything less sounds…well, *uncomfortable*.

There's also the tiny problem that I'm not, and never will be, in love with Peter. Do not misunderstand—I love him dearly. But not like that. I've seen him break far too many hearts to ever give him mine.

I'm opening my mouth to object when he cuts me off,

his eyes shining. "Before you say no, let me kiss you, just once. How else will we know, Sophie?"

Instead of butterflies, I get a mild case of indigestion. Boys are fun to flirt with, and some are certainly nice to look at, but I've never found one I want to get close to.

"Come on," he murmurs, already moving in. "Just one kiss."

"Peter, you are the worst sort of cad," I say, but I don't push him away this time.

It might be magical. He's right—how will I know if we never try?

"All right. Go on." I clench my eyes closed, waiting with dread.

Instead of a kiss, I'm answered with a laugh. "You look like a frog, Sophie. *Relax.*"

Immediately irritated, my eyes fly open. I'm about to say something scathing, but Peter moves in, and his mouth meets mine.

And it's fine, I suppose. He smells nice enough—like the lavender his mother uses in her soap. His lips are soft but firm, and he certainly knows what to do with them.

It's not unpleasant. I could do it again if I had to. Maybe this is it. Maybe Peter and I are supposed to be together.

He backs up, meeting my eyes. "Well?"

"You're very practiced," I say wryly, earning a bright smile from him.

"Marry me, Sophie. Let's run away together."

I think about it for several long seconds, and then I nod. "Yes, all right. But it will have to be soon."

Peter grins and yanks me against him, kissing me again.

"Sophia!" a man bellows.

Peter and I leap apart, and my eyes widen in surprise when I find Father on our side of the willow tree, looking angrier than I've ever seen him.

And to be honest, I've made him angry plenty of times, so he must be livid.

I smooth a wrinkle in my sleeve. "Hello, Father."

Someone must have seen me.

Peter gulps, looking properly terrified.

Father bristles at my nonchalant tone and levels me with a stare that could curdle milk. "Peter and I are going to have a discussion. You will go home. *Now.*" He narrows his eyes. "And Sophia—"

He's using my full name—that's never a good sign.

"—if you're not there when I arrive, so help me…"

It takes me precisely twenty-three minutes to walk to our manor. It takes Father thirty-one. Which means I have at least eight minutes to track down the sorry sibling who tattled on me before he arrives.

I shoot Peter an apologetic look and turn toward the street. If I hurry, I can likely shave several minutes off the walk.

As I silently seethe, I debate which one it was. My older sisters, Rynn and Eva, used to be my first choices, but Rynn is in Farthendale and Eva's busy setting up her new home.

That leaves my younger siblings. Elisette usually has her pretty nose buried in a book, so I doubt it was her.

Besides, she rarely wanders the streets. She tends to attract suitors, though she doesn't have much use for them.

Elisette's twin, Martin, wouldn't care enough to say anything, and Penny's not the tattling sort.

That leaves Anneliese.

I throw open the front gate, startling several chickens. They flap about, squawking in the most obnoxious way. I cannot stand our ridiculous assortment of animals. Not only do they smell, but they're messy and time-consuming to tend.

My family has money—plenty of it—yet my parents insist we keep livestock on the grounds like we're common country folk. It's humiliating. I'll gladly marry Peter, just to escape it.

A goat looks up, blinking his glassy eyes at me as he slowly chews a mouthful of fencepost. I glare at him and march up the front steps.

"Anneliese!" I yell as soon as I'm through the doors.

My voice echoes through the halls, startling a scraggly cat Rynn brought home several years ago. It's an awful beast, and ugly as a creature can be. She glares at me from around the bookcase, probably plotting my death.

Elisette appears on the landing, book in hand. "What's the matter?"

"Did you tell Father I was with Peter?" I demand.

"You were with *Peter?*" She blinks at me with disbelieving green eyes—like she simply cannot believe I could be foolish enough to continue seeing the tailor's son. "After Father forbid it?"

"Yes." I wince, not wanting to admit the next part, but I must tell someone. "He kissed me."

"You let Peter kiss you?" she says, aghast. "Did you have to wait in line?"

It would be funny, but I'm not sure it's a joke.

She's about to jump into one of her lectures, and I hastily say before she can begin, "Never mind. I know Liesa told Father. Tell me where she is."

"I haven't seen her."

I yell for Anneliese again, and this time Penny makes an appearance. My youngest sister walks down the stairs, as calm as you please, until she's in front of me. She and Anneliese are twins, and they are almost perfectly identical. Penny, however, has unusual, but striking, amethyst eyes. I personally think she's prettier than Anneliese, but that's probably because Anneliese is a snotty, attention-hungry brat.

"She's not here," Penny says, but whether that's the truth or she's just protecting her twin again, I have no idea.

Before I can interrogate her further, Father storms through the doors. I turn to him, my mouth agape. For him to make it back this quickly, he must have practically run.

"Sophia, into my study." He marches past me without another word.

"That's not good," Elisette says, and then she winces when I glare at her.

I follow Father, resigning myself for another lecture.

As soon as I'm in the study, he slams the door and

stalks to his desk. "This is the final straw, Sophia. You're getting married."

"I know." I straighten my spine, preparing for the argument. "I'm going to marry Peter. We talked about it before you arrived."

My chest tightens in the most uncomfortable way, but I ignore the sensation. I can marry Peter—there's no one I like more.

Father narrows his eyes and all but ignores me. "I finalized the arrangements yesterday. Milton asked for your hand, and I have spent the last few days speaking with him and his parents." His eyes soften. "They're good people, Sophie. Milton will take care of you—you'll live a comfortable life."

"Milton is a farmer!" I exclaim, past horrified.

"He is a landowner," Father snaps. "He is a good man, who makes an honest living."

I don't care if Milton's a good man. He smells like sheep, and his hair sticks up in all directions, making him resemble a scarecrow.

"I won't marry him," I swear.

Father narrows his eyes. "This is not up for discussion, Sophia. I was willing to let you find a good match on your own, but time after time you've proven yourself to be less responsible than your older sisters."

My stomach clenches when I realize he's serious.

"Please don't do this," I beg.

"It's already done. We'll make the announcement in the morning."

I try to breathe, but it's as if the air isn't there. My

lungs ache; my world spins. It's happening too fast, and I don't see how I can talk Father out of it by morning. The noose is around my neck, and soon, it will be too late.

We have no choice. Peter and I must leave.

Tonight.

CHAPTER 2

I sneak down the street, staying in the shadows where I can. It's a new moon, perfect for slipping away.

It's almost midnight, and I managed to leave the house without running into anyone. I don't expect them to realize I'm gone until morning.

The tailor's house is just ahead, in a quiet district with manicured gardens. The man has done well for himself in Astoria's capital city, catering to the nobles and their many fashionable whims, and his family wants for nothing.

I know Peter's home almost as well as my own. His bedchamber balcony overlooks the distant northern mountains—the best view in the house, he likes to boast. Fortunately for me, it's also the one with the balcony next to the largest tree on the property.

I hop over the decorative half-wall that separates the house from the street and cautiously make my way to the rear of the manor. The walkways are narrow, and the beds on either side of the path are lush with plants. Carefully, I veer off the cobblestones and head to the tree. I can climb it to reach Peter's balcony, as I've done a dozen times.

As soon as I'm off the walkway, the smell of basil drifts to me. I must have disturbed an herb garden. It's a strange daylight smell, something you don't expect in the dark of night, and it reminds me to be more careful where I step.

I reach the tree and test my weight on the lowest branch. The oak is old and sturdy, and the limb barely moves. I scamper up the tree, using my boot-encased toes to dig in while I pull myself up with my arms. The bark digs into my palms, but it's a familiar sensation, one I don't mind in the slightest.

Mother used to say I would have made a better squirrel than a girl.

Just when I'm halfway up, fully-surrounded in the tree's thick canopy of leaves, but not yet high enough to reach Peter's balcony, I hear voices.

I freeze, not daring to even breathe.

"Do you have to leave?" a girl says from the balcony above, her words breathy and overly feminine.

"I'm afraid so, darling," a familiar male voice says. "It's time I see the world. But know I will think of you every moment I am gone."

Peter.

"Can't I go with you? I'll leave, Peter. I'll go wherever you go."

It only takes me three full seconds to place the voice.

It's Thelma, the baker's youngest daughter. She's a year older than I am and as dimwitted as she is pretty.

I peer through the lace-pattern of leaves above, just in time to see Peter kiss Thelma. I'm not surprised, and I'm not even hurt—it's Peter, after all. But I'm still overwhelmed with the desire to break off one of these branches and throw it right at his fool head.

After I tamp down that urge, I find a more comfortable position and wait for them to leave. After several more minutes, I hear a door opening, and the two disappear into the house. Faint music drifts from the room, but it's silenced when the door swings shut.

Apparently, the tailor is having a party, one Peter didn't invite me to. But of course he didn't. He had a few loose strings to tie up before we set off on our grand adventure.

Once the pair is gone, I crawl onto the balcony, find a chair in the corner of the chamber, and wait.

At half-past midnight, Peter comes waltzing into the room, whistling quietly as he tosses his jacket aside.

I clear my throat, scaring him half to death. He jumps like a frightened cat, and I smirk. "Thelma, Peter? Really?"

He winces. "Saw that, did you?"

I nod. "I'm afraid so."

Wasting no time to make amends, he kneels in front of me. "It was a goodbye, Sophie. I meant every word I said earlier—let's go, let's see the world together. You mean more to me than a thousand other girls, and you know it."

"I know you're acquainted with a thousand girls, so you certainly have plenty to compare me to." I smile to ease my words and lean forward. "I'm leaving tonight, but I couldn't go without saying goodbye."

Peter exhales slowly. "You're mad at me."

"I'm not." I'm not sure I should tell him I expected no less. "But I'm not going to marry you."

After letting the words soak in, he groans.

"I don't blame you." Then he flashes me a grin. "I wouldn't marry me either."

I begin to stand, but he grabs my arm. "What do you mean you're leaving?"

"Father wants me to marry Milton."

"The farmer who lives by the river?" he exclaims.

"That's the one."

Likely tired of kneeling at my feet, Peter pulls me up as he stands. "But he's a bore. I had a conversation with him once. He didn't even notice when I dozed off."

"Father wants to announce our engagement in the morning, and I can't do it."

Peter looks at me earnestly, concern written all over his face. "Let me come with you—you can't go alone. It's not safe."

"No, you stay here." I raise an eyebrow. "Thelma needs you."

He nods sagely. "And Liza and Mary and—"

I shove his chest, and then I pull him into a hug. He wraps his arms around me. It's a warm and friendly embrace—infinitely better than the kiss we shared earlier.

I'm halfway out the door when he sets his hand on my shoulder. "Find adventure, you hear?"

I smile. "I will."

His expression softens, shadows with a hint of worry. "Promise me you'll take care of yourself."

"I promise, Peter."

And then I'm out the door, climbing down the tree, and scurrying into the night.

I'VE BEEN WALKING for two hours, twenty-seven minutes, and fourteen seconds. It's almost three in the morning. I'm cold, my feet ache, and I have no idea where I'm going.

It becomes clear I should have thought this through a little better.

At precisely four-o-one, I give in. I find a nearby log, plop my sorry self onto it, and loudly say, "Oh, great fairy godfather Mortimer. I, a stupid human, humbly need your magnificent and wonderful magic."

Five minutes and twenty-two seconds later, the root of all my family's blessings and curses appears before me with a bang.

"Hello, Morty." I stick my legs out in front of me, stretching as I look at the cantankerous man. He's of medium-height and build, perhaps a bit on the slender side. His brown hair, peppered with gray, has a light wave to it, and it's receding ever-so-slightly at the temples. All in all, he's a rather average man.

Oh, and he also has wings.

"How are you this evening?" I ask him.

The fairy sputters, looking very much like a perturbed goose. He points at me, his eyes narrowed and oh-so-livid. "*You.*"

I raise my hands and motion to the farmland around me. The mountains are still far, far away. "I've found myself in a bit of a predicament."

"If I remember correctly, little wicked one, you weren't supposed to call on me after I helped Eva."

I shoot him an incredulous look. We both knew that wasn't going to happen, whether Mortimer will admit it or not.

Wise enough to know it's a dead-end conversation, he changes tactics. "Do you realize it's four in the morning?"

"Of course I do," I say sweetly to my family's very own fairy godfather. "Thanks to you, I know exactly what time it is, every moment of the day."

That's my blessing. Horrid, isn't it? Elisette gets all the luck. Mortimer made her devastatingly beautiful, and what does she do with it? She bemoans her fortune and hides all day with her books.

Mortimer stares at me with such loathing, I briefly wonder if he's going to turn me into a rock. The only thing that protects me is his fairy council. I believe they'd get fussy if the reluctant godfather maimed the humans he's been charged to bestow gifts upon.

"What do you want?" he asks, fighting for patience.

It's strange how I seem to have that effect on the men in my life.

"Since it took you two minutes longer to show up than usual—"

"You *woke* me in the middle of the night, you wretched beast of a gir—"

"I had time to think." I lean forward. "How about you

give me magic, and then I won't have a reason to pester you anymore."

I might have called him a time or two, just for the fun of it. It gets rather dull being the third-born, especially when there are four younger children—all of them between me and what could have been a delightful baby-of-the-family status.

"Even if I could give you magic, I shudder to think what kind of havoc you would cause with it."

"Ah, Morty. I love you too."

He's like our very own crotchety uncle, the bumbling kind whose gifts are often more like hurricanes than blessings. Deep down, however, I think he cares for us. For some of us, he might have to dig a little more. From the look he's giving me, I have a feeling I'm at the bottom of the trench.

"Again, I repeat, *what do you need?*" he snarls.

What do I need? What *don't* I need? Everything is a right fine mess. If I don't want to end up as a farmer's wife, I can't go home.

"A knight in shining armor," I mutter to myself, and then I say to Mortimer, "I need—"

"A knight, you say?" he cuts me off, his eyes strangely focused.

"I meant it in the most figurative way."

"For once, bothersome, Wicked One—"

Wicked One—that's his nickname for me. It's sweet, don't you think?

"—You might be the answer to *my* trouble."

No words uttered prior to this moment have struck more fear in my heart. I know that look in his eyes—it doesn't end well. Bad, bad blessings are gifted when Mortimer wears *that* expression.

I stand abruptly. "Mortimer, no. Listen to me—*listen.*" I draw the word out and make him meet my eyes, talking to him almost as if he were a naughty, distracted dog. "I need a cloak, new sturdy boots, and a hefty bag of gold. Nothing else."

I would have liked him to whisk me to the closest inn, but I don't dare ask for that now.

"You'll like Henri," he muses as he studies me with narrowed eyes. "But I'm not sure Henri will like you…"

"I will not like Henri!" I protest.

Of course, I have no idea who Henri is.

Then I pause. "*Why* wouldn't he like me exactly?"

Mortimer nods, mostly to himself. "Two birds with one stone. Come along."

And before I can do a thing to stop it, my world goes bright white. I've never been transported with fairy magic before, though I hear it's excruciating—possibly the worst thing you could live through.

People who say that have not listened to Elisette drone on about the life cycle of a silk caterpillar.

I gasp for breath when the harsh, unnatural light subsides. After a moment, I peer around me. It's still dark, but it takes me no time to realize we're not in Astoria anymore.

The air smells rich, like dense forest and hundreds of years' worth of fallen evergreen needles. Firs tower around the meadow Mortimer has plunked us down in; they're menacing shadows in the dead of night.

"Where are we?" I ask, surprised to find my words come out as a croak.

"Briadell." Mortimer adjusts his long robes and starts forward, stalking toward the trees.

I hurry to keep up with him. The last thing I want to do is get lost in the northernmost mountain kingdom. Well, technically it's not the *most* northern. That honor belongs to Elsland, the troll kingdom at the very top of our map.

"Briadell?" I demand, shivering in my lightweight gown. "Why in the world would you bring me here?"

The fairy doesn't bother to answer me.

"Mortimer!" I glance around, uneasy. "Briadell is wild! There could be animals out here."

He chuckles, but it's not an assuring sound. "Oh, there are. Wolves, mountain cats...bears."

I stumble over an exposed root. "Where are we going?"

But he needn't answer. The trees open, revealing a lake and a tall, statuesque palace that sits on a peninsula in the middle of the water.

I stop dead in my tracks, refusing to go any farther. I'll take my chances with the wildlife.

Mortimer shoots me a hassled look over his shoulder. "Are you coming or not?"

Folding my arms over my chest, I look him right in the eyes. "Not."

Briadell's true royal line is cursed; everyone knows it. Few have seen their current prince, and they likely never will. He is a recluse, a hermit. His features are twisted, and his eyes are said to be black, depthless pits. The mountain kingdom's prince is as ugly as the land is beautiful.

At the gnarled prince's demands, a duke rules in his stead, overseeing the kingdom from the small city of Dathpore, near the Farthendale border. Without the help of its prince, Briadell makes a living exporting timber and gold from their plentiful mines, and few people bother to give him as much as a thought.

He is but a tale, one older children tell young ones to frighten them.

I was never scared of him, not ever. But now? Cowering in front of his palace in the dead of night? I'm properly spooked.

Mortimer looks as if he's about to physically haul me to the castle when something behind us catches his eye. He looks beyond me, and I whirl around, not about to let something sneak up on me in the dark.

A shadow approaches, someone human. I edge behind Mortimer, hoping his magic will save us. If it doesn't, at least I'm confident I can outrun the old man.

"Mortimer," a deep voice says. "Why have you returned?"

"I'm here to grant you your blessing." The fairy grabs my arm and not-so-gently yanks me forward. "I've brought you a wife. Please, keep her. I assure you, I do not want her back."

"Mortimer!" I exclaim.

"You must understand, this is out of my hands," Mortimer explains to me in the most impartial way imaginable. "Henri saved a goat from a ravine—"

"It was a girl," the man interrupts. "Not a *goat*."

"And the council assigned him to me as punishment for—" Mortimer stops abruptly. "That doesn't matter. All you need to know is that Henri is a knight looking for a bride, and you are a girl looking for a knight. Congratulations. Do not expect a wedding present—I won't be sending one."

And just like that, the fairy disappears.

CHAPTER 3

"Mortimer?" I say. When he doesn't answer, I call his name again. Well…I less "call" and more "yell."

The fairy does not return.

A breeze blows through the trees, and I hug myself, trying to stay warm. It's even colder in the mountains than it was in Astoria. I eye the shadowed man and tell myself there's no reason to fear him. It doesn't matter that he's a complete stranger, or that we're alone in the dark, next to a castle that makes regular appearances in children's nightmares.

He's probably very nice.

True, it's disconcerting that I can make out very little of his appearance in the dark, but there are a few details I file away. Henri is tall, and he has a nice enough voice. Judging from it alone, I assume he's probably twenty-one, maybe as old as twenty-five.

"He gave me a ridiculous summoning poem," Henri

says after several long, tense moments. "But I don't remember it."

"Oh, great fairy godfather Mortimer. I, a stupid human, humbly need your magnificent and wonderful magic," I recite. I've said it a hundred times; I know it by heart.

"That's it."

"I've already used it today. He never answers me twice in a twenty-four-hour period. Once, he ignored me an entire week."

Henri lets out a single, throaty laugh, and I shiver, again remembering how alone we are. If I could only see him better…

"You're cold," he says.

"I'm fine."

"There's no reason to stand outside." He starts toward the castle. "We'll find a solution to this in the morning. I apologize for Mortimer all but kidnapping you on my behalf."

I watch him, aghast. His apology barely registers. "You live there. With *him?*"

The man stops, and his shoulders go rigid. "I live alone."

It takes several moments for his words to sink in. Once they do, I let out a tiny peep and stumble back.

"I see you've heard of me," he says, disdain—and something else—heavy in his voice. He bows, but it's a mocking gesture.

"You're Prince Henri?"

There's a long pause before he finally answers. "I am."

How can that be? The prince should be over forty years of age. The man before me is nowhere close to that.

"Mortimer said you were a knight," I accuse, still walking backward in the dark.

"I was a knight—saved damsels in distress, slew dragons, all those sorts of things. But that was before my family...passed."

My anxiety kicks up a notch. "That was twenty years ago."

With a low growl, Henri continues toward the castle. "Time moves quickly when you're cursed."

I look over my shoulder, ready to run, but something stops me. Mortimer wouldn't have brought me here if it were dangerous—would he? As much as he'd like to be rid of me, he surely wouldn't risk the wrath of the council. And Henri, supposedly *the cursed prince of legend*, saved that little girl. Why would a monster do that?

"Wait," I call. On impulse, hoping my intuition isn't leading me to a terrible death, I run to catch up with him.

He glances down at me. "Did you decide the forest was a bigger threat than I am?"

"I'm not fond of animals." Somewhere distant, a wolf cries, and I cringe. "Especially ones with large teeth."

Henri stops dead in his tracks and stares at me. "What's your name?"

Something in his tone makes me gulp. "Sophia."

The prince bends close, but I still can't make out his features in the dark. "Well, Sophia, you should have stayed home."

His words are colder than the night air. They strike my

core and make me wonder if it wouldn't be safer to take my chances in the forest.

Then another wolf howls.

Henri continues toward the palace, leaving me to chase after him like a puppy.

"How can you be the prince?" I demand, careful to keep my eyes averted. My mind is playing horrible tricks on me, and I'm terrified what I'll find if I look at him too closely in the dark. "His father died over two decades ago."

"I'm aware of that."

Henri's voice no longer carries the gentle tone it did earlier, and I sorely miss it.

"How old were you when he passed?"

The prince stops again. "Do you always ask this many questions when you first make a person's acquaintance?"

"Usually," I admit.

We cross an arched, stone bridge and walk under the portcullis. I look up, half-expecting the iron spikes to come crashing down.

"If you won't answer my first question, answer me my second," I say, needing to fill the silence. "How old are you now?"

"It's irrelevant. I stopped aging the day the curse was cast."

His somber mention of the curse sets me on edge. "Who cursed you?"

There has been much speculation on the subject, but the general consensus is that the royal family doomed themselves—took into their possession an enchanted item that brought them far more harm than good. But I've always wondered if it wasn't a troll. The monsters' kingdom is so close to Briadell, and they are sneaky creatures.

Jealous of our way of life, they spell themselves to look human and occasionally travel into the lower kingdoms, causing turmoil. They always have a tell, however—a massive wart on their forehead or eyes that are too close together. Those sorts of things.

"It doesn't matter," the prince says, finished with the subject.

I follow him into the palace, grateful for the respite from the frigid night. Then I come to an abrupt stop.

"It's colder in here than outside," I murmur under my breath.

And darker.

I look around, searching for Henri in the pitch-black room. The door closes behind me, and I whirl around, looking for its outline. Nothing.

What have I done?

The darkness closes in on me, squeezing my lungs, forcing me to accept that I've walked into a nightmare of my own making. I knew the stories, and yet I followed the cursed prince into his palace like a lamb ready for slaughter.

Just as I'm ready to scream at Mortimer, demand he come back at once, a tiny flame flickers in the dark. I watch it, half-mesmerized as the fire grows. Light blooms in the room, spreading through the stone entry, illuminating the modest space.

"There are fireplaces in nearly every room," Henri says from in front of the fire, kneeling at the hearth with his back facing me. "Our summers are cool, and our winters are brutal."

I study him in the low light, aghast. Under the heavy cloak he wears, he appears to have a handsome build. His hair is so blond, it looks white in the firelight. He begins to turn, and I immediately avert my gaze.

His footsteps echo in the formal entry, growing louder as he walks my way. I don't dare look at him, so I keep my eyes on my feet. I hug myself, trembling as much from fear as the chill.

Henri steps around my back, and I clench my clasped hands. Something heavy and warm settles around my shoulders, taking me by surprise. His cloak smells just like the forest, and it's much too long. It pools around my feet, making me wonder just how tall the cursed prince is.

"I won't hurt you." Henri stops just in front of me. "If that's why you're suddenly as silent as a mouse."

I study his boots, which are now in my line of sight. They're scuffed from wear, and a dried layer of mud cakes the edges. They look nothing like the boots a prince would wear.

"Why won't you look at me?" he asks, his voice oddly curious.

In answer, I only shake my head.

After several moments, he places the tips of his fingers on my chin and tilts my jaw up. I close my eyes, refusing to look.

"You're terrified," he murmurs, lowering his hand. "Why?"

"Because right now, at this very moment, I can imagine you are a normal man, with a normal face. Once I lay eyes on you, I won't ever be able to pretend again."

He's silent for several seconds. "Sophia, open your eyes."

His words are abrupt, and they are laced with irritation…and possibly a sliver of amusement.

Slowly, knowing I can't keep them closed forever, I open one eye, taking the slightest peek, bracing myself for the worst.

Then I open them both, somehow let down. "You're not a grotesque monster."

Henri's mouth tilts with what might be a smile. "I'm sorry to disappoint you."

It's still dim in the room, but his features are clear. He has a strong jaw that's shadowed with heavy blond stubble. His nose is straight and perfectly proportioned, and his eyes are light and deeply set under full brows.

He looks like a warrior—a true knight, solid and muscular. And so very intimidating.

"You said you were cursed," I say.

"I am."

"You don't look cursed." I wrinkle my nose and let my eyes wander over him. He's a bit of a disappointment, to tell you the truth.

Where are the horns and tusks? Where's the fur or boils?

Henri crosses his large arms, studying me. "You are a very strange girl."

"I've heard that before, though the adjective is usually different." I can tell he wants to ask, so I put him out of his misery. "Infuriating, incorrigible, insolent—a lot of 'I' words. Mortimer prefers wicked, but he's difficult like that."

The prince gapes at me, and I clear my throat and turn away from him. "This is a nice...entry."

I grimace at the gaudy tapestry hanging on the wall opposite the large entry doors. It depicts a woman in a low-cut gown, standing in a battlefield, sword in hand. Her enemies lie at her feet.

"Very...colorful," I add.

Henri steps next to me and crosses his well-muscled arms. He scowls at the tapestry. "My stepmother."

"You don't have a stepmother," I say, and then I bite my tongue. He would probably know better than I.

Arms still crossed, he gives me a wry look. "I did. Very briefly." Then he frowns and returns his attention to the tapestry. "I still do, I suppose."

"Did she escape the curse?" I ask, because I just can't seem to help myself.

He looks at me again, wearing that same amusement-laced, slightly exasperated half-smile. "She cast the curse."

One second goes by, then two.

Finally, I say, "*She was a troll.*"

The words come out as an excited whisper. Excited not because I'm happy his family was cursed...but because I was right.

Henri nods slowly. "She is."

"Is?"

"She's alive, somewhere."

"How do you know?"

He lets out a short, mirthless laugh. "Because I'm still under her curse."

Even though the room is growing warm, and Henri's cloak is heavy and lined with fine, thick fleece, I shiver again.

I'm quiet for several moments, trying desperately to curb my questions.

"What was her tell?" I finally ask, deciding that's a safe topic.

"She didn't have one."

I step around his front so he must face me. "They *always* have one."

Henri leans down, meeting me at eye level. "Been around many trolls, have you?"

Startled by how close he is, I blink. For a cursed prince, he's very handsome. Not in the same way as Peter, who is lean and almost lanky. Henri is a warrior, through and through. Strong. Tall. Imposing.

And I realize as I stare into his light eyes, I like that about him.

Very much.

"No," I say, my voice the slightest bit breathy. "I have not."

The prince's eyes narrow momentarily, almost as if I've startled him. He watches me for half a heartbeat more, and then he pulls back abruptly. "You must be exhausted. It's nearly dawn."

Which reminds me. "Why were you walking in the woods in the middle of the night?"

Ignoring my question, he says, "I don't have a guest

suite prepared for visitors, but you may sleep in my chamber tonight."

Under his cloak, I set my hands on my hips and stare at him.

Real humor lines his face, making him look even more rugged. "I'll sleep elsewhere, of course."

I nod.

He lights a candelabra, and then he motions for me to follow him. Away from the fire in the entry, the palace is freezing. I eye Henri's lightweight muslin shirt and toy with the edge of his cloak. "Aren't you cold?"

"Not particularly."

I open my mouth to argue, but then think better of it.

He leads me into the chamber, and I hesitate by the door. His bed is massive, made of dark wood and covered in burgundy linens.

This feels very wrong.

Henri turns back, and the flickering candlelight casts dancing shadows on his face, making him look eerie. "Sophia."

That's all he says, just my name.

Nodding, I shuffle into the room.

Satisfied, he sets the candelabra on a side table and turns to the fireplace. Soon, a fledgling fire crackles in the hearth.

"I'll be gone from morning until dusk." He moves for the door, but before he goes, he turns back. "Tomorrow evening, we will discuss what must be done with you."

"Done with me?" I ask, almost laughing.

Without answering, he walks out the door.

"Wait!" I call.

Reluctant, he turns.

"Don't you want the candelabra?"

A ghost of a smile plays over his lips. "I have excellent night vision."

And then he's gone.

Light streams through the tall, dappled glass windows. I blink several times, burying my face in the covers as I turn from the bright sunshine.

Then I freeze.

The linens smell like fir needles and freshly-cut wood. The scent instantly wakes me, and I sit up. Gray, flaky coals lie silent in the hearth. I have no idea how long I slept, but judging from the height of the sun, it must be late. I swing my legs off the bed and attempt to straighten my sleep-wrinkled gown.

Mortimer.

"Oh, great fairy godfather Mortimer. I, a stupid human, humbly need your magnificent and wonderful magic," I all but snarl.

Seven minutes pass, then eight.

He's not coming. It hasn't been long enough, and he's still ignoring me.

"Fine."

Cautious, I open the door and step into the hall. It's obvious Henri's stepmother put her unique touch on this part of the palace as well. Garish paintings line the walls; all of them depict the same woman in various poses. Her eyes seem to follow me, and I hurry through the hall, trying to remember my way.

I find myself hopelessly lost, wandering down stairs and up stairs, into towers and out of towers. The entire time, I don't see a sign of life—human or otherwise. There are no cats or dogs, not even so much as a single mouse. In most of the rooms, furniture is covered in white sheets. The decor that's unprotected is layered in dust.

By the time I find my way to the palace's entry, I'm practically jogging. The silence is disturbing. What happened to all the servants? The maids and cooks and stewards? Has everyone truly left Henri?

The grand palace is a shell of a structure, haunted by the memory of something terrible in its past.

I don't make a conscious decision to leave, but when I see the enormous double-door entry, I run for it.

Outside, late afternoon sunshine greets me. It kisses my face, wrapping me in familiar warmth. I step forward, walking out onto the huge courtyard balcony that overlooks the sparkling lake.

A duck family swims near the shore, carefree.

The forest scene is idyllic, and it's teaming with life. Several squirrels chase each other in the brush, and tiny swallows dive for the water, snatching gnats from the surface.

Slowly, I turn to study the palace. It's tall, with graceful spires and balconies, but no birds sun themselves on the turrets or railings.

Twenty-year-old flags flap in the summer breeze, their sapphire fabric sun-faded and torn. A once-handsome crest hangs in shreds over the massive entry, giving the palace an unsettling look.

The general feeling of abandonment hangs heavy in the air.

Spooked, I jog down the steps, eager to be away from the palace, at least for a while. I travel the overgrown peninsula trail, heading toward the forest. The towering trees don't look as intimidating in the light of day. In fact, they're breathtaking.

There are cobblestones underfoot, but the native vegetation has taken over, growing between the stones and pushing them apart. Years ago, this was likely a heavily traveled road, groomed for carriages and carts.

I pause halfway down the peninsula. A village sits in a nearby valley. A tiny wisp of smoke rises from a chimney, telling me there are people still living there. Hope blooms in my chest, and I hurry that way.

I run the whole way to the tiny town, and I'm exhausted once I pass the protective wall. A few villagers loiter about, and every eye falls on me as I walk the dusty streets.

"Have you come to gaze upon the palace?" a woman calls from a wooden porch.

Startled to have been addressed, I turn to her. "I'm sorry?"

Her hair is gray and streaked with a few lingering black strands. She wears it in a tidy bun at the back of her head, and tiny spectacles sit on her pert nose. She goes back to her embroidery. "Our village should have withered when the royals were cursed, but we survive on the travelers who dare gaze upon the forlorn palace."

I bite my lip, glancing at the towers that are just visible over the trees. "Do you ever see the prince?"

The woman shakes her head. "Never, not since my children were young. The palace is empty. No one comes, no one goes. Poor Henri died with his father, I reckon."

"Then why does it sit empty?"

She looks up, meeting my eyes. Her gaze is strangely knowing, and for a moment, I almost think she's realized I'm no ordinary traveler amusing myself with the local legend. "Many gawk, but none dare enter."

My lips twitch at her dire warning. "You must be very brave to linger in a village so near."

"We have our protection." She holds out her cloth, beckoning me forward.

"A bear?" I look up after studying the embroidered cloth.

"The bear is our guardian." She begins to stitch again. "None in this village have been harmed by the curse since he arrived. We see him often, though he never leaves the trees."

A cold chill passes through me. Just what is the bear protecting the villagers *from*?

"He's white?" I ask, looking again at the design.

"As white as snow."

"Why do you stitch him?"

"We do it to show our gratitude."

"On a handkerchief?"

"On all our linens and clothing." She smiles. "But the handkerchiefs we leave at the edge of the forest as a gift. In the morning, they're always gone."

It's sweet, I suppose, but I find the idea of a giant bear prowling the woods more than a little disturbing.

"What are you thanking him for with this particular handkerchief?" I ask.

She knots the thread, apparently finished. "He saved my granddaughter when she fell down a nearby ravine—carried her safely home on his back."

CHAPTER 4

I'm still reeling when the woman hands me the handkerchief. "Perhaps you can take this for me?"

"I..." I stammer, stepping back. "I don't know how to find the bear."

Her sharp eyes spark with amusement. "I didn't say you did. I was hoping you could leave it at the forest's edge, save me an uphill walk."

Gulping, I accept the offered token. I'm sure she notices how my hand shakes. "All right."

She jerks her chin in the direction I came from. "Go on now, the sun will set soon. You don't want to be in the forest after dark."

"Because of the bear?"

She smiles. "Because the woods are treacherous to navigate."

Of course.

I give her a nod, wondering what kind of mad place Mortimer abandoned me in, and turn back to the woods.

The woman is right; I don't want to walk through these trees after the sun sets. It's already low in the sky, and the shadows are growing long.

Smoke from cooking fires in the village wafts through the air, mingling with the scent of the evergreens. It's a welcome, homey smell and a sharp contrast to the eerie stillness of the trail.

Handkerchief in hand, I hurry for the palace, only because I have no other place to go. I refuse to look at the swatch of fabric. Several times, I swear I see a flash of white fur in the trees. But that might be my imagination playing tricks on me.

As I walk, I repeat my plea to Mortimer. Again, he ignores me.

I reach the peninsula just after the sun sinks below the horizon. Color leaches from the forest as dusk settles, turning the dusty green trees gray. I pull open the heavy door, but the entry is dark.

Something about the lonely, dim palace seems infinitely more frightening than the balcony overlooking the lake. Instead of lighting a fire in a dust-riddled sitting room and huddling by it until Henri returns, I hurry out the doors, back into the fresh mountain air.

As dusk turns to dark and the air goes from cool to cold, I whisper Mortimer's summon a dozen times. Even if he were to simply wait with me, at least I wouldn't be alone.

For the first time, I miss the chaos of home. It's never quiet, not with the nine of us and the livestock. Something or someone is always making noise, even in the dead of night.

But here…nothing. Even the ducks have gone silent.

I should have gone inside, waited by the fire, braved the empty shell of a palace.

"Sophia?"

I nearly jump out of my skin when I see Henri walking up the steps. He's so quiet, I didn't hear him approaching.

"What are you doing in the courtyard?" He opens the doors, and his shadowy, human form ushers me inside.

"The palace is too quiet," I whisper.

Hugging myself, I wait for Henri to start a fire in the entry hearth, just as he did early this morning. Soon it's crackling, bringing much-needed warmth to the room.

"I went to the village today." I clasp my hands, trapping the handkerchief between them.

"That's a long walk," he says in a conversational tone. "Would you like to wait here by the fire or join me as I light the rest?"

"I met a woman."

"I imagine you did. Roughly fifty percent of the villagers are women." He holds up a stringer of fish. They're good-sized, but they look small in comparison to his large frame. "You must be starving. I realize I left you with nothing to eat. As I'm sure you can imagine, it's been a long time since I've had a guest."

He's avoiding the conversation, and I let out a flighty laugh that's a product of frazzled nerves. "She gave me a handkerchief."

Henri finally drags his gaze to mine.

"To give to *you*," I say.

"Sophia—"

"That's your curse." I step forward. "You're the white bear who looks after the villagers."

A mask falls over the prince's face, but his eyes flicker with pain before he schools it. "The curse backfired."

I step closer, irrationally wanting to comfort him. "What do you mean?"

He shakes his head, obstinately mute.

"It happened over twenty years ago," I say. "Have you ever talked about it? To anyone?"

Silence blankets the room. It's so stifling, I wonder how it doesn't suffocate the fire.

Henri turns his back on me, and now I know I've done it. I've pushed too far, made the bear angry. He's probably going to eat me.

"The troll's name is Amara, and she's the queen of Elsland. She came shortly after my mother passed, worked her magic, enchanted my father. As soon as they were wed, she plotted to kill him so she could claim Briadell as her own."

I'm so shocked by his words, I can't answer.

"She cast her deadly curse, and I leapt in front of it, trying to save him." He pauses. "As a baby, a fairy gifted me with protection. The fairy magic thwarted Amara's curse, twisted it into something entirely different. Instead of a monster, I became the guardian bear. As long as I hold this form, my kingdom is safe from her. She cannot step foot in Briadell."

It's beautiful in a way, and so very sad.

"And your father?"

"I couldn't save him. He died that day."

Slowly, worried he's going to shy away, I walk toward

Henri. I place a soft hand on his back, hoping to offer comfort even though I know it's not enough.

I've lived for amusement. I've never experienced loss—I've never even wanted for anything. And Henri…his life has been full of so much pain.

The prince tenses when I first touch him, but his muscles gradually relax under my palm.

After several minutes of quiet companionship, I softly ask, "Why did Mortimer bring me?"

Henri still has his back to me, making the conversation easier.

"Because it's a lonely life," he says, and then he turns his head, meeting my eyes. "And the council knew my one desire."

My throat goes thick with emotion. No one has ever made me *feel* before. I blink quickly, hating the way my eyes sting. Softly, I say, "A maid?"

He lets out a startled laugh, just as I desperately hoped he would, and it makes my world right. It's a happy sound, loud and joyful. It warms me from the tips of my fingers, all the way to my toes.

Finally, he turns. I offer him the handkerchief. He takes it, running his hands along the embroidery as if it's precious.

"How many tokens do you have?" I ask. Twenty years is a long time.

"Nearly a hundred."

I drop my hand, feeling awkward now that he's facing me. "Why then is this the first time the fairies have sent someone to help you?"

"It's not." His mouth tilts in a wry smile. "But it's the

first time I couldn't convince them to leave it alone—though the first fairy was almost as belligerent as Mortimer."

We share a smile, and my reaction scares me. *This*—this is how it's supposed to be. My heart beats like a hummingbird in my chest, and my stomach flutters. I'm hot and cold, and I feel weightless—like I could float away.

Why, *why*, is it that when I'm finally feeling the pull of genuine attraction, the man ends up being a *bear?*

"The coach visits the village tomorrow," Henri says, his eyes warm. "I'll send you with a satchel of money—however much you think you'll need to get to Astoria."

Wait a moment.

What did he say? I was so busy cataloging my reaction, I must have missed something vital.

I blink at him. "Astoria?"

"To wherever you live. I assumed from your accent you are Astorian."

"You're sending me away?"

Didn't we just share a moment? Even a tiny one? *Something?*

"You belong with your family, Sophia." He almost looks reluctant, but that's probably wishful thinking on my part. "You have to go home."

"Or I could stay."

He studies me for several long moments. "You would marry me, knowing what I am?"

Gently, I pull the handkerchief from his hand and hold it between us, making a statement. "I will gladly marry the man who's earned almost a hundred of these."

"You'll marry a bear?" he presses.

I gulp. A bear.

Marry a bear.

Can I marry…a bear?

No matter how I phrase it, it doesn't get any better.

Mother will faint when she hears the news, and Father—oh, he'll be livid. I can just see the way his face will turn red, how he'll rant and rave because I chose this path—my own path—instead of playing the good daughter and becoming a farmer's wife.

Then I think of Peter, how he'll laugh when the news eventually reaches him.

Will I marry a bear?

"Yes, Henri. I will."

CHAPTER 5

*D*ark, thick clouds mask the stars, blocking their dim light. Henri makes his way through the forest, his steps nimble for such a large man. We walk side-by-side, close but not touching, and the silence between us is as heavy as the moisture-dense air.

I open my mouth half a dozen times, trying to think of something to say to break the tension. And half a dozen times, I stop myself.

At a distance, a bolt of summer lightning cuts a jagged line through the sky. The thunder reaches us several moments later, but the storm is headed our way. It's only a matter of time before the worst of it is directly overhead.

"How far to the village?" I finally manage.

"We'll reach it soon," Henri answers just as I trip on a rock in the trail.

I stumble forward, but before I can regain my balance, Henri catches my arm and pulls me to his side. My breath catches in my chest as I wait for him to release me.

Instead of setting me free, he keeps me close, guiding me the rest of the way.

Just as the forest opens, revealing the village in the valley, the wind picks up. It yanks on my cloak and pulls strands of hair from my braid.

"Where do we go?" I ask Henri, raising my voice to be heard over the storm. Another bolt of lightning lights the sky, this one much closer.

"To the tavern," he hollers back, pulling me down the deserted street.

We locate the wooden building standing in the center of the square and push through the doors.

Most of the tables are full, and the patrons turn to see who just barged into the room. Henri closes the door behind us, shutting out the storm.

His face is shadowed under the hood of his cloak, hiding his identity from any who might recognize him after these long twenty years.

"Welcome, travelers," the bartender calls from behind a long, scarred bar at the rear of the room. "We have mulled wine, venison stew, and plenty of mead. Find a place to sit, and we'll be with you shortly."

Henri nods and leads me to a small table in the corner of the room. We're near the fire, but safe from its dancing light. Nervous, both for Henri and for the reason behind our late-night outing, I slip into the seat facing the room.

Henri takes the one opposite me, keeping his back toward the villagers who continue to cast curious glances our way. "We'll wait out the storm."

"Do you think anyone will recognize you?" I say, careful to keep my voice low.

"No," he murmurs, lowering his hood. "But it doesn't hurt to be cautious."

Again, I'm reminded of what a lonely life Henri must have led, keeping himself apart, prowling the woods and watching over the very people who fear him.

A young maid, not a day older than Anneliese, sets steaming mugs in front of us. Her eyes flutter over Henri with appreciation, but there is no recognition in her expression—and how could there be? He was cursed several years before she was born.

The thought makes my stomach knot. Though he looks young, Henri's older than I am—has lived twice my life. Does he think I'm foolish and naïve? Is that, perhaps, why he fought Mortimer like he did? Maybe he didn't want to marry a puppy, someone who has experienced so little.

"It's not too late to change your mind," he says as soon as the girl leaves.

My eyes fly to his, and my cheeks heat with embarrassment. "It's not too late for you to change yours either."

The straight line of his lips twitches, the corner of his mouth tugging up with suppressed amusement. "Are your parents cruel? Is that why you left them?"

"No, it's nothing like that." Finding it difficult to hold his gaze, I lower my eyes and take a sip of the hot spiced wine. "They are kind and simple people—caring, generous. I love them very much."

Saying the words aloud, hearing them leave my mouth, makes my heart twinge. I *do* love them—all of them. And leaving is hard. I'll miss Rynn's comforting guidance and Eva's smiles. I'll miss pretty Ellie continually droning on about her books, Martin pretending to be brave, Penny's sweet, down-to-earth presence, and Anneliese's flamboyance. I'll miss pestering Father and finding Mother in her garden.

But I must live my own life.

"There must be some reason I can't coax you to go home," Henri says, just as I knew he would eventually. "Why are you here?"

Again, our eyes lock in the dim light of the sleepy tavern.

"With me," he finishes, his tone softer.

My stomach flutters with nerves and something more. And before I can stop myself, my story spills out. I tell him of Father's heroic deed that turned my parents' lives upside down and brought us Mortimer, and of my sisters, brother, and our life in Torina.

"And this Milton," Henri says when I reach the end, long after our drinks are gone and our bowls are clean. "He's not a good man?"

"He's a fine man, I suppose. Dependable, steadfast..."

Henri frowns, but his eyes are laughing. "You make those sound like bad traits."

"Not bad, just *dull*."

The prince's answering smile is bright and unexpected, and it does funny things to my chest. "I was right—you are a strange sort of girl."

I sit back in my chair and cross my arms. "Finally rethinking the wisdom of this, are you?"

He tosses several pieces of gold on the table—far too many pieces for the meal—and gently tugs me up by my arm even though the storm continues to rage outside. "No, but I know now we must exchange our vows quickly, before you realize I'm as dull as your farmer."

His hand lingers on my arm for several moments after I rise.

"Is that your way of telling me that you're dependable and steadfast?" I tease as I crane my neck to look up at him.

"I'm afraid so." With a wry tilt of his eyebrow, he steps closer. "Both those and more."

And though I'm rather skilled at banter, my brain goes blank as my chest grows warm.

"We should..." I nod toward the door, almost breathless.

Along with handsome and built like a rock, the cursed prince is charming. It's probably for the best he's also a bear—if he weren't, he'd be far too perfect.

THE VILLAGE ELDER doesn't seem pleased to find us knocking on his door several hours after dark, but he's appeased by the impressive pouch of gold Henri wordlessly hands him from the doorstep.

"And this can't possibly wait until morning?" the man asks, though he's already peeking inside the bag and motioning us inside.

"We can't linger in the village," Henri says smoothly, lowering his hood with a guarded expression.

The elder, a man of middle years with a soft, rounded

stomach and graying temples doesn't give Henri so much as a second glance.

"Seen the castle and now you're finished with the village?" The elder shoots us a knowing look. "Off for the next thrill?"

In response, Henri only gives the man a cryptic shrug.

"Fine," the elder says, tucking the pouch away. "Let me draw up the papers. Make yourselves comfortable."

He motions to an upholstered bench by the fire and disappears into the back room. We wait in perfect silence, listening to the sound of the wind and the crackle of the pine logs burning in the hearth.

Exactly twelve minutes later, the elder appears with a rolled parchment and a pair of spectacles on his nose.

Motioning us to the table, he unrolls the parchment and hands a quill to Henri. "Sign here, if you will."

Henri nods and makes quick work of the document, signing with such flourish there is no possible way a person could read his name.

"Now you, Miss," the elder says, handing the quill to me.

My hand trembles as I sign my name under Henri's. I've barely lifted the quill from the parchment when the elder snatches it from my hand, blows on the signatures, and rolls it back up, tying it with a thin ribbon.

"Now," he says, his tone all business. "Do you have rings?"

I begin to shake my head, but Henri produces a pair from the inside pocket of his doublet. They're beautiful, obviously old, and likely worth a fortune.

The elder frowns, possibly following my same line of thought. With furrowed brows and an expression that makes him resemble an inquisitive owl, the elder turns his gaze on Henri.

The prince doesn't so much as flinch under the man's scrutiny, and eventually, the elder brushes off whatever thought was troubling him and nods. "Very well."

It's a simple ceremony—if you could even call it that. I'm so overruled by my nerves, I barely hear the words the man speaks.

"I do," Henri says solemnly.

"And do you, Sophia, take this man to be your husband?"

Here it is, the moment of truth. There's no turning back, no more pretending this is a lark and nothing more.

I meet Henri's eyes, more terrified than I've been in my life.

The prince watches me, his eyes conveying his understanding. "It's your choice," he whispers, barely loud enough for me to hear.

"I do." There's conviction in my voice. I don't just say the words; I *mean* them.

We exchange rings, the man congratulates us and shakes Henri's hand, and then we're gently, but *insistently*, pushed out the door, into the cold, turbulent night.

"Have we gone the wrong way?" I holler over the wind.

Lightning flashes around us, lighting the trees. They

tower over us, their branches like great, grasping claws, reaching for us in the bursts of light.

Henri grasps my hand tightly, pulling me with him at a fast pace. "No, we're heading for shelter."

I follow him without question, mostly because it's impossible to carry on a conversation in the storm. Rain comes down on us with a vengeance, stinging as the droplets pelt against our skin. We cut through thick brush, and my long, borrowed cloak catches on twigs and brambles. Wet, slimy grass catches around my ankles and slick mud cakes my boots, making it difficult to walk.

Just when I'm about to ask if we're near our destination, a bolt of lightning illuminates a sheer rock wall ahead.

I stop abruptly. "I'm not going in there!"

The cave looks ominous in the light of the storm—the type of place where bats and wolves and old, gnarled witches would abide, waiting for their next meal.

"It's safe," Henri insists, tugging me when I refuse to move.

Another crack of lightning—this one so close, the thunder booms even as light illuminates the sky—makes me leap forward.

I follow Henri into the cave, grateful to find it's shallow, leaving no place for unwanted creatures to linger unnoticed.

Once safe from the storm, Henri runs his hand over my shoulders. "Your cloak is drenched."

"How long before the storm subsides?" I ask, looking at the forest beyond.

Henri's silent for several moments as he joins me,

staring out at the storm. "I'm not sure. I think the worst of it is over us now."

A freezing gust of wind that's far too cold for summer blows into the cave, and I shiver under the cloak.

"You're cold," Henri says, his voice heavy with concern and what sounds an awful lot like shame.

I turn to face him. "My dress is dry under the cloak, and the cave is sheltered. I'm all right."

He doesn't answer, and I search for him in the cave. Except when the lightning races across the sky, it's too dark to make out so much as his silhouette. Needing to know he's near—needing to know I'm not alone even though in truth my new husband is a stranger—I reach for him. My unease lessens when my fingers brush against his cloak.

Immediately, Henri takes my hand in his. His skin is chilled from the weather, but his grip is comforting.

I never imagined I'd be standing in a dark cave in the dead of night, with a storm raging outside, on the day of my wedding.

But strangely, it's all right. I set out, looking for adventure, and that's precisely what I've found.

"Sophia?" Henri asks after nearly an hour in the cave. The storm is finally moving out. The thunder has grown distant, and the rain is now a gentle patter on the grass outside.

"Hmmm?" I turn toward him, wishing I could make out his face.

He doesn't answer right away. Just when I think he's chosen to stay silent, he says, "Out of all the girls

Mortimer could have chosen, I'm glad it was you he dragged to my castle."

His words are quiet, and somehow, I know he wouldn't have uttered them by the light of a fire.

Now grateful for the dark, I squeeze my new husband's hand. "I am too."

CHAPTER 6

It's harder than you might think to write a letter to one's parents, announcing your surprise newlywed status. It's even harder to explain that their new son-in-law spends his daylight hours as a wild animal.

I tap the quill to the parchment and nibble the inside of my cheek. Finally, I finish the letter and ask my parents to send my love to all my sisters and Martin. Before I lose my nerve, I quickly write at the end, *PS: The palace is very nice, and when the sun is up, Henri turns into a bear.*

Yes, that should do it.

Satisfied, I seal the parchment with my new crest. It looks very official.

"Oh, great fairy godfather Mortimer," I recite. "I, a stupid human, humbly need your magnificent and wonderful magic."

Three minutes and twelve seconds later, the fairy appears.

"Oh, fabulous time, Morty!" I exclaim, hoping to get a

rise out of him. "That was exactly two minutes and ten seconds faster than your last visit."

The fairy scowls at me. "You're keeping track?"

"I don't want you to think I don't appreciate your gift."

"What do you want, little nuisance?"

"That's *Princess* Nuisance now." I hold out the letter. "I need you to take this to my parents."

He narrows his eyes. "Do I look like a delivery service?"

A delightful retort is right on my tongue, but I do need him to take the letter since I don't dare go to the village, so I choke it back and bat my eyes. "Please, Morty? It's just a little letter. Besides, don't you want to tell them what a good job you've done? After all, you are very clever for introducing me to Henri. I believe that should be acknowledged, don't you?"

He rips the note from my hand. "Do not think you've tricked me. I know exactly what you're doing."

I try—but fail—to hide my smile.

Without another word, he disappears.

Sighing, I glance around the empty sitting room. As sad as it is, I wish the fairy had stayed a little longer, perhaps given me news on my family. I'd even be happy to let him prattle on about the strange inventions he tinkers with.

Henri's off, doing things bears do, and I'm here, bored to death. We've been married a week.

Looking back, I'm surprised no one in the village asked questions. But, then again, no one has laid eyes on their prince for twenty years. They didn't suspect a thing when they saw the handsome young knight.

Twenty years.

I didn't want to dwell on it before, but now it haunts my every waking moment. I'll grow older, but Henri will remain stagnant.

And what about children? Will we have any? *Can* we have any? And if we do…will they be *cubs?*

It's a truly horrifying thought.

Pushing the worries away, I spend the day by the window, waiting for dark. I've already wandered the palace, taking down every awful tapestry, painting, or sculpture of that troll woman. They're all piled in the ballroom, ready to be burned at Henri's first convenience.

Earlier in the week, I was so desperate for entertainment, I stooped to tidying up the palace, room by room. I've done laundry and dusted and mopped, and I still haven't touched half the castle. I'm afraid by the time I finish, I'll have to start over again.

At this point, I'm so desperate for entertainment, I'd relish the chance to tend a flock of chickens. Of course, we probably can't have livestock because my husband would be tempted to snack on them.

I walk about the room, lighting dozens of candles, waiting.

Waiting.

Finally, at twelve minutes past sundown, I hear the echo of Henri's boots on the wooden floor outside the sitting room. I leap to my feet, ready to greet him with the enthusiasm of one of those tiny, obnoxious, ankle-biting dogs.

The prince walks through the door, carrying the scent of the forest on him.

"Sophia." As he has every evening since we've been wed, he sets his hands on my shoulders and presses a kiss to my forehead. The first time, I thought he missed my lips because he's so tall and obviously out of practice after twenty years as a recluse.

Now I've resigned myself to the fact that he's doing it on purpose.

It's a strange thing, this being married to someone you barely know. I always thought I'd marry for love—imagined someone like Peter, I suppose. Someone with bright, sparkling eyes and wild ideas.

Instead, I've yoked myself to a serious man who is silent for long stretches at a time, often broods, and makes my stomach flutter every time he walks through the door. A man who's reluctant to so much as touch me.

If our situation were typical, if we met under everyday circumstances, I doubt Henri would look my way. His slow smiles would be for lovely, bookish Elisette or sweet, responsible Penelope. He wouldn't want troublesome Sophie, the sister with the freckles across her nose because she spends too much time in the sun, the one who can pick locks and climb trees and beat all the boys at every card game known to man.

Maybe that's why he won't touch me. He enjoys my company, but I'm not what he wants in a wife.

Henri sits in a chair by the fire, staring into the flames. "How was your day, Sophia?"

I choose the seat next to him. "I wrote my parents a letter."

A smile plays at his lips. "You finally worked up the courage?"

I nod.

"Is that all?"

"I took down your stepmother's art."

His eyes light with amusement. "All of it?"

"Everything I could reach."

Along with the fire in the hearth, the candles cast the room in gentle light. The juxtaposition of the soft ambiance and his hardened lines do something strange to my chest.

"I'll help you remove more of it tomorrow evening," he promises and then looks back at the fire.

Irritated with the distance between us, I rise from my chair and stop in front of him. "Henri, I had a thought."

The prince watches me with cautiously amused eyes, wondering what I'm going to say.

Steeling my nerves, knowing he might push me away, I lower myself to his lap, sitting on the very edge of his knees. He goes very still, but his hands settle on my waist as if on instinct.

The fact that he hasn't nudged me away gives me courage.

Before I speak, I mentally organize my argument. Wary, Henri swallows. For a split-second, his eyes drop to my lips, and then he rips his gaze back to my eyes. "What's your thought?"

My stomach clenches. The husky tone of his voice almost makes me forget my words. If my nearness has this effect on him, then *why* has he been keeping me at arm's length?

It takes me a moment to clear my head, and then I pull myself together. "You said you know your stepmother is alive because you're still under the spell, correct?"

He tenses at the mention of the troll, which is not at all what I want. Softly, with butterflies swirling in my stomach, I place my hand on the side of his neck.

Oh, this strategy is going to backfire. Instead of trying to sway Henri with my feminine wiles, I'm becoming distracted by the curve of his lips and the quickening rise and fall of his chest.

"Yes," he answers absently.

Focus, Sophie.

He's going to say no; he's going to tell me I'm foolish and naive.

I clear my throat and try to give him my most reasonable look. "What if we travel to Elsland…and slay her?"

Henri's eyes go wide with shock. His grip on me tightens, and he laughs, surprised. Once he composes himself, he leans a margin closer. "You're rather blood-thirsty for a pretty thing, aren't you?"

I lower my eyes as my cheeks go hot. I'd like to say it's from girlish embarrassment, but it's not. I'm flushed from our nearness and irritated he thinks the idea is foolish.

And all right, it *is* a bit ridiculous. But the thought of living out our lives, waiting for that monster to finally die a natural death? It's not terribly appealing.

When I don't answer, Henri tilts my chin up so I have no choice but to face him. "I've thought about it too, believe me. The first ten years, I was consumed with the idea of justice. She killed my father—Briadell's king. She committed treason against my kingdom, and she should pay for her crimes."

"What happened?" I whisper.

Henri shrugs. "I never found her. She lives in a remote palace in Elsland. I've been told it's a lonely structure far to the north, located east of the sun and west of the moon. There are no roads to the castle, no path. Without the help of magic, a person can never find it."

"There has to be a way."

His thumb brushes my jaw, making me shiver. "Are you so unhappy with me, Sophia, that you're already restless after only a week?"

He's lowered his voice again, and if he's doing it on purpose, he should stop unless he means to follow through.

"No," I answer, and it's the truth. I'm not unhappy with Henri. I just want more.

"Good." His grip tightens on the sides of my waist, and he places me on my feet as he rises. "I brought more fish. Are you hungry?"

Not for fish.

Hiding a sigh, I nod and follow him from the sitting room.

"Oh, great fairy godfather Mortimer. I, a stupid human, humbly need your magnificent and wonderful magic."

Seven minutes later, the fairy appears, looking a wee bit angry. "You! Always *you!* What could you possibly need now?"

"It's a pleasure to see you as well."

"What do you want?" He bites out every word, fighting to stay composed.

I sit on a rug on the stone floor of the great ballroom, my gown spread out around me like I'm five years old. "I just wanted to say hello. See how you are."

The fairy growls and holds up his hand, looking very much like he's about to wink out.

"It's too quiet here," I say, my voice sounding small even to my own ears. "And lonely."

Growling like I've told him I need him to save a basket full of kittens from a wolf, he lowers his hand. "Aren't you happy with Henri?" He motions to the grand room. "With the palace I've given you? I've made you a princess, and still, you aren't content."

He marches over to me and sticks his finger in my face. "This is why fairies shouldn't meddle with humans. No matter what we do, you will always find something to bemoan."

"Can you lift Henri's curse?" I ask abruptly. "Mortimer, I promise I will never call you again…if you just take it away."

Mortimer lets out a long, drawn-out sigh and does the unexpected. He gathers his robes and sits on the floor in front of me, cross-legged like a child. "Sophia—"

My mouth falls open, and I gape at him. "Did you just use my name?"

Mortimer bristles.

"You *know* my name?"

"I can leave…"

I shake my head, silently promising to be good.

"I cannot lift a troll curse."

"But Henri said the fairy blessing he received when he was born is what counteracted the troll's curse in the first place!"

"And it turned him into a *bear*," Mortimer reminds me, looking very taxed to be having a civil conversation with me. "Our magic doesn't mix well. It's like oil and water, repelling the other. The results are unpredictable at best."

I lean forward, making him meet my eyes. "If any fairy can do it, it's *you*. Mortimer, you are a terrible, *terrible* fairy godfather, but you are an excellent inventor."

The fairy thinks about it, looking very much like he wants to decline, but his mind is already working. "Maybe if I..." Then he shakes his head. "No."

"Please—*help me*."

After several long moments, he levels me with a questioning stare. "Your family resists my magic at every turn, and yet you're begging for my services. Why?"

I give him a slow smile. "Because I'm not afraid of a little chaos."

He stares at me for several long seconds, and then he shakes his head curtly. "You're no longer my problem. You are married—I've done my part." Then he stands abruptly and wipes imaginary dirt from his robe.

Resigned, I flop onto my back and stare at the elaborately painted ceiling.

"Wait," I call before he leaves. Listless, I roll my head to the side to face him. "If you see my family, will you at least tell them I miss them?"

"Homesick?" He raises a brow.

Though I want to argue, I nod.

Without another word, he's gone.

I turn my face to the ceiling again, acknowledging it's probably for the best. Mortimer's never gotten anything right, not in his life. But I have no one else.

Twenty minutes later, a knock echoes through the palace. It's the strangest sound, loud and insistent. Someone's at the main entry.

Who could be calling?

I don't even know if it's safe to answer, but I'm so starved for human contact, I run the whole way, stopping to straighten myself only once I reach the entry. Pasting a huge smile on my face, I toss the door open, only to find a box.

It's wrapped in ribbons and tied with a bow. I pick it up, bringing it inside, surprised to find it strangely unbalanced. Frowning, I read the note.

For old time's sake. To help with your homesickness.

With trepidation, I untie the bow. There's the strangest noise coming from inside, almost like the hiss of a—

I scream as the lid flies from the box, and a black and gray blur of scraggly fur goes tearing down the hall, hissing and spitting the entire way.

Grabbing my chest, I gasp for breath. Once I feel as if I'm not going to die of shock, I growl into the air, "Thank you very much, Mortimer."

The wretched fairy brought me Rynn's worthless cat.

CHAPTER 7

With a groan, I roll over. Blinking, I let my eyes adjust to the dark room. The fire burned out during the night, and it's cold enough to make me believe it's early morning. I'm not sure what woke me.

I'm just about to pull the blankets up to my chin and go back to sleep when a thought occurs to me. It's almost dawn.

My nerves hum with nervousness as I push the covers aside and walk across the room to check the window. I open it, bracing myself for the crisp morning air. The horizon is just lightening.

I need to hurry.

Quickly, I tame my hair. I found several gowns in wardrobes scattered throughout the palace, and I pull one on now. It fits well enough, better than some, but most importantly, it's black.

I tiptoe into the hall. Henri's been sleeping in a southern wing, far from my chamber in the north. My heart beats wildly, and I second-guess myself the whole way across the palace. Two times, I almost turn back to my room.

But I must see for myself.

Henri's door opens just as I turn down the hall, and I dart behind a tapestry. It's dusty back here, and who knows what insects might be lurking.

The prince's door shuts, and I hear each footstep as he turns the corner to pass me. I hold my breath and stay as still as possible. It's not the first time I've sneaked around in the dark, but it's the first time in the palace, and I'm not sure what Henri will do if he catches me.

Once his footsteps fade, I gingerly slip out from behind the tapestry and make my way down the hall. Henri doesn't leave out the grand front entry. No, this time he chooses a side entrance that leads to what, at one time, was likely a kitchen garden. Now it's just a sad tangle of mint and weeds.

I slip out the door behind him, careful to keep to the darkest of shadows. In fact, I'm quite proud of myself. I don't think I've ever been this stealthy.

"I know you're back there, Sophia," Henri says from ahead of me as he reaches the edge of the overgrown garden. He turns, peering at me through the dusky light of early morning.

So much for stealthy.

Hesitant, I walk forward.

He crosses his arms. "Why are you following me?"

I give him a one-shouldered shrug.

"Gregarious in the early hours, aren't you?"

After a moment, I let out a long breath. "I wanted to see for myself. See that you're actually…"

"A bear?"

Wincing, I nod.

"All right." He takes off his cloak and then kicks off his boots.

I take a step back. "What are you doing?"

The words come out as a squeak.

Henri looks up. The sun is nearing the horizon, and the sky grows lighter by the minute. "How many bears have you seen wearing clothing?"

A nervous giggle escapes me, but I clamp my mouth shut. "I've never seen a bear, so I couldn't tell you."

He tosses his boots and cloak into a crate near the wall and walks toward me. "Go inside, Sophia. You don't want to see me change."

I realize now he was trying to intimidate me so I'd leave.

"Is it painful?" I ask, though I don't really want an answer.

"Yes."

"I'm sorry," I whisper.

He sets his hand on my shoulder. "Go inside."

"Can I see you after?" I focus on the contrast of the cool morning and the heat of his hand. "When you're…" I can't bring myself to say it. "Furry."

Henri chuckles, and then he winces. I step back, afraid he'll shift right in front of me.

"Wait in the kitchen until the sun crests the horizon, and then you may come back to the garden."

"Is it safe?" I ask, second-guessing the wisdom of my little morning outing.

"If you change your mind, I will not blame you."

I begin walking backward, toward the side entrance. "Will you know me? When you're a…"

"*Bear*, Sophia."

"Yes, *that*."

He cringes again, and I hasten my pace, hoping I don't trip.

"I'll know you," he promises just as I dart inside.

I close the door behind me and clench my eyes shut. This was a terrible idea—I'm not going back out.

Yet for some reason, I linger in the kitchen like I'm unsure. I poke around things, looking for enchanted kettles or pots to pass the time, but I find nothing unusual.

Finally, the sun rises past the trees and illuminates the eastern windows with warm light. I can go out now. Henri will have changed.

I edge toward the door.

I'll just take a peek—I'll stick my head out, gaze at the bear standing in the tangle of now-wild raspberry canes, and that will be that.

Slowly, I crack the door.

"It's fine, Sophia," Henri calls from nearby.

Shocked, I step out the door, and then I scream and flatten myself against the wall. My legs begin to tremble and then my hands follow.

The bear is massive, white as snow, and very…

Bearlike.

"You're all right," Bear-Henri assures me. "I'm not going to hurt you."

"You can talk!"

He gives me a look, one that is disturbingly human. "Yes, I'm aware of that."

"*How?*"

"I learned at a young age, not long after I began walking." Then he wryly adds, "You could say I was a prince prodigy."

My laugh gets caught in my throat.

Slowly, he starts toward me. The sunlight catches his fur, making it gleam. He'd be very majestic-looking if he were not my husband. Of course, if he were not my husband, he would probably eat me.

"Henri," I start to edge toward the door. "I can't."

But that doesn't stop him. He continues toward me, walking at a steady pace as if trying not to frighten me. "I'm me, Sophie. Just me."

He called me Sophie. Something about the endearment makes my shoulders relax marginally.

"You *are* scared of animals, aren't you?" he asks, his unnaturally blue eyes trained right on me. "Is that the problem?"

I inch a little farther away, following the wall. "I'm not scared of all animals. Only large ones—in particular, the carnivorous kinds with sharp teeth and claws."

He's right in front of me now. I could reach out and touch him if I so desired. My fingers twitch against my will—because I am certainly *not* going to try it.

"It's all right," he says in a voice that's incredibly disconcerting. He sounds exactly the same. "Go ahead."

"I'm..." I clear my throat. "I'm fine. Thanks all the same."

His eyes spark with amusement. "And I thought you were brave."

I purse my lips, trying not to laugh. That was a low blow.

Steeling my courage, I extend my hand. One little touch, that's all. Just a little pat on his shoulder.

My fingers slide into his fur, and I inhale sharply. His coat isn't as soft as I expected. In fact, it's quite coarse—not like a horse's mane, but certainly not like a bunny.

Henri watches me with eyes that are disconcertingly *his*.

Slowly, I pull my hand back.

"Well?" he asks.

I finally dare to meet his gaze, though I don't think I'll ever get over the shock of seeing him like this. "You make a very fine bear."

A laugh rumbles from his great chest, and I press against the wall once more. Apparently finished, he turns to leave. "I'll return at sunset."

And though he's terrifying, I hate to see him go.

He looks back over his shoulder. "Unless you'd like to walk with me?"

I bite my bottom lip, thinking far too hard.

Looking disappointed, Bear-Henri nods once and continues without another word.

"Wait," I call before he's past the garden wall.

He stops and peers at me once more.

Taking a deep breath, I step forward. "I'll come with you."

As pleased as a bear can be, Henri waits for me to join him.

CHAPTER 8

Another week goes by, and then a month, and then several more. Soon, Henri and I slip into a routine—a lonely routine, but comfortable for the most part.

By day, my husband wanders the forest, tenaciously protecting the nearby villagers from everything from wolves to careless accidents. I join him occasionally, but I've grown bored of aimlessly wandering the woods.

At dark, he returns to me. We usually share a simple dinner of greens I've gathered from the forest and whatever meat Henri brings back. I miss baked goods, but I don't dare venture back to the village for supplies to fill the larder.

As far as the villagers know, we traveled through near the beginning of summer and are far, far away.

With the passing of months, Henri and I become friends. I treasure the time we spend together. The sun has become my enemy, and the moon is dear. Still, in all this time, Henri has not touched me past the kiss I receive on my forehead every evening when he returns home.

And I am going mad.

Henri sits across from me now, in front of a crackling fire. He's reserved tonight, more so than usual.

We've eaten and are enjoying the pleasant hours before we retire to our chambers—him in the guest suite and me in his room. Why he continues to separate himself even though we are married, I'll never know.

Rynn's wretched cat appears out of nowhere and leaps onto his lap. Henri absently scratches her head, and she purrs, reveling in the attention.

For the first time in my life, I wish I were a cat.

As if sensing my irritation, the awful beast turns her head to face me, giving me the feline version of a smirk.

"You're quiet," I say to Henri as I glare at the cat.

He turns, meeting my eyes. "Are you happy, Sophie?"

The question takes me by surprise. "Yes, I'm fine. Why do you ask?"

Shaking his head, he looks back at the fire. "You're vibrant, lively, and I've trapped you in this empty palace, all so I don't have to face the evening hours alone. It was cruel of me."

I narrow my eyes, wondering where this is coming from.

After several long, quiet minutes, he finally says, "A woman in the village died today. The entire community wept at her funeral. They spoke of all the things she'd done in her life, all the people she cared for. She'd touched every one of their lives in some way."

"Henri—"

He turns to face me, his eyes searching mine. "And I realized I'm going to lose you someday. You're going to waste your life here, shying away from the sun, and for what? I'll be here long after you're gone, burdened with the memory of what I've lost. And you'll never live."

He's right. But I wouldn't leave him now, not ever. I've grown to care for the hurting prince, more than I thought I would. More than I thought I could.

"I'm here by choice," I remind him softly. "And I stay by choice."

Needing him to understand, I set my hand on his. For the most part, I've respected the distance he seems to crave. I tease him occasionally, flirt a little, but I never let him see how I'm truly starting to feel.

I suppose I've been frightened—frightened of the bear, frightened of the man. Perhaps even more the man because he keeps me at such a distance.

The contact startles Henri, and he pulls his arm back quickly, inadvertently bumping a tray of pillar candles burning next to him. The cat yowls and leaps to the floor.

The tallest candle tips, spilling wax. I quickly set it right, but melted wax has already pooled on the table.

"Careful—" I begin, but it's too late. Henri sets his elbow right in it.

"Did it burn?" I ask, tugging his arm toward me so I can get a better look.

"No." He grimaces and shakes his head, disgusted with himself. "But I liked this shirt."

I laugh under my breath. "I can clean the shirt."

Henri looks up, meeting my eyes. The nearness takes me by surprise, and my mouth goes dry.

"It's impossible to remove tallow wax from fabric," he murmurs, his voice deeper than before.

My stomach clenches, and my breath catches in my throat. "Impossible for some, perhaps. But not me."

Feeling bold, and maybe a bit reckless, I loosen the ties of his leather jerkin.

Henri tenses and places a hand on mine, stopping me. "Sophia."

It's a quiet chastisement, one that would have made me cower when I first arrived. But I'm not afraid of him anymore, and I'm done living like strangers.

Softly, I bat his hand away and continue my work.

His arm falls slowly, and he swallows. His reaction makes my heart race, makes me wonder why he's stayed away all this time.

I tug the jerkin over his head, and then I begin to untie his shirt's neck laces.

"Sophie," he says again, this time sounding pained.

It's the tightness of his voice that makes me pause. I meet his gaze, unsure what I'll find there. Once I look, I wonder if I should have kept my head lowered.

There is wanting in his light eyes, a desire to be close. But there's conflict there as well. He wages an internal battle, but I have no idea what it might be.

"I cannot clean your shirt if you don't give it to me," I point out, trying to keep my voice even. The words come out quiet, but at least they don't waver.

Henri's breathing is shallow, matching my own, and he

shakes his head as he clenches his hands in an attempt to keep them to himself.

The simple movement is like lightning to my chest.

Pretending I am brave, I step into him, moving as close as I am able. Even seated, Henri's imposing. He dominates the chair, makes it look dainty even though it's constructed of heavy wood.

I set my hand on his shoulder, and he tenses. Then, giving in, he closes his eyes and lets his head fall back. "You can't do this."

"I can't touch your shoulder?" I ask, purposely obtuse. I let my fingers drift down his arm, my touch light and exploratory. "Or your arm?"

A smile dances across his face even though he's at war with himself. "You are wicked."

"What about your elbow?" I ask, biting back a giddy smile as my hand drifts farther. The wax is already drying, making the fabric rigid. I lean close to him, willing him to open his eyes.

He finally complies, giving me a wry look when his stare meets mine.

Nodding, breathless and drunk on the sensation of touching him, I lean closer, softly teasing, "That's surely allowed."

Perhaps without him realizing it, his hands move to the sides of my waist. "You have to stop."

"Then why are you pulling me closer?" I whisper.

He tugs me against him, destroying the wall he's so carefully built between us. I stumble, startled, and catch my balance on his chest. There's no sensation more exquisite than Henri's arms around me and the steady thrum of his heart beating under my palm.

"Because I am a fool," he breathes against my neck. "And this is torture."

I close my eyes as his lips skim my jaw, cheeks, temples, and nose. But never my mouth.

"Why won't you kiss me?" I demand after several long, agonizing minutes.

"I cannot."

My hands rove his shoulders. "It's really not that difficult," I tease as his lips move to the sensitive skin behind my ear. "I think you'll see if you give it a try."

"Sophie," he says, my name a caress and a plea. "If you care for me, please stop."

I pull back, making him meet my eyes. "I do care." I voice the words solemnly, though they aren't enough. "Henri, I care very much."

He cups the back of my neck, his expression earnest. "Then do not ask me to kiss you. I am not strong enough to resist again."

Unnerved by the intensity of his gaze, I slowly nod. "All right."

"I mean it, Sophie," he says, his tone too serious for my liking.

A lump forms in my throat. I try to pull away, but Henri holds me in place, not letting me leave.

"You don't have to go," he whispers.

"But you just said—"

"I know what I said, but that doesn't mean I can't hold you and wish things were different."

I soften against him. His eyes are haunted, and I want

nothing more than to take the look away. What has him so worried?

Nodding, I catch his hand and pull him from the chair. Without a word, I lead him to his chamber. Though we cannot be together, we are married. I finally see he needs me as much as I need him, and I do not intend to spend another night alone.

Henri resists but finally lies on the bed, pulling me close. "I have to leave before the dawn," he murmurs into my hair.

"That's for the best," I say lightly, reveling in the sweet feel of his arms around me. "I don't particularly want to share my bed with a bear."

His rumbling laugh makes me smile, and I lie here, utterly content as I listen to the rhythmic sound of his breathing. It soon slows, and I know he's fallen asleep.

I turn in his arms, gazing at his face in the meager moonlight that spills from a part in the drapes. "I'm afraid I'm falling in love with you," I whisper, safe because I know he can't hear me.

It's a terrifying thing, something I didn't plan on.

Softly so I don't wake him, I press the gentlest of kisses to his lips.

Henri made me swear I wouldn't ask him to kiss me, but I never promised *I* wouldn't kiss *him*.

A BIRD CHATTERS outside the window. Its song is so foreign, I wake with a start. Not once in the entire time I've been here have I seen a bird on the palace. They grace the nearby trees and forage for food in the meadows, but they do not venture near the castle itself.

I sit up, startling the man next to me. Henri groans, still half-asleep.

Sunlight washes over him, illuminating features I've never seen in the warmth of morning.

"Henri," I gasp.

He opens his eyes, wincing as they adjust to the light. He stares at me, seemingly bemused, and then he bolts upright in the bed.

"No," he says, horrified as he scans his body—his human body. "*No!*"

Startled by his strange reaction when I believe he should be rejoicing, I shrink away from him. He turns to me, his face etched with horror...and fear.

The fear scares me, but my brain is muddled. Henri is handsome by firelight, but in the day...

How is this man my husband?

Henri's magnificent. His features are chiseled—a marble artist's dream in flesh. But it's his eyes that capture me. They're ice-blue, just like the bear's. It's a color that was impossible to ascertain in firelight, and they are trained right on mine.

"Sophie, what have you done?" he whispers as he yanks me into a tight embrace, clinging to me in anguish.

"I don't understand," I say against his chest.

He nudges me back and meets my gaze. "You've broken the curse."

"And that's *bad?*"

"She'll feel it, and she'll come. Briadell's no longer

safe." His frown darkens. "You have to leave—you have to go home."

I shake out of his grip. "I *am* home."

"I can't lose you," he says, his voice urgent. "Sophie, she'll hurt you out of spite."

Hugging myself, more terrified than I want him to know, I shake my head, adamantly refusing. "I'm not leaving you."

He clenches his eyes shut. "What is that ridiculous summon?" His eyes fly open, and he recites Mortimer's call. But he says it wrong, and I'm not about to correct him.

To my great surprise, moments later, the air crackles, and the fairy appears.

Except it's not the fairy at all.

"Amara," Henri snarls as his muscles go rigid.

The woman is tall and regal, with ebony black hair and a look of pure loathing twisting her stunning face. She cackles as if mad and points a slender finger at Henri. "I knew it was only a matter of time."

He pushes me behind him, about to say something, when the woman gasps. Her body flickers, almost as if half of her is trying to wink back to whatever forsaken place it is she came from. After a moment, she gains control, and then she turns her venomous stare on the prince. "I will kill you slowly, and then I will rule your kingdom as its queen."

She raises her hand, and green, wispy magic crackles in her palm. Before she can cast it, I throw myself in front of the prince.

The pain is horrible, and I hear myself scream. It stabs

like ice, jolts like lightning, and comes in waves, rising and falling like the tide. I writhe in pain, desperately wishing I could faint just so the misery would end. And through it all, my wretched blessing keeps track of the time. Three seconds pass, then five, seven, ten...

"Save her, and I will do anything you ask," I barely hear Henri say.

"*No*," I manage to gasp out, but that one word is all I have in me.

"Anything?" the troll woman demands.

"Anything you ask," Henri vows, "*if you save her*."

The pain comes to an abrupt stop, and I go still on the bed. The memory of the magic courses through my body, making me numb—and thankful to be. Silent tears run down my cheeks, but I'm helpless to stop them.

"The wretched fairy magic lingers," the troll snarls to herself, flickering again like the flame of a candle.

It doesn't look as if she can stay much longer. Soon, what's left of Henri's original, troll-twisted childhood blessing will shove her from the kingdom.

She turns her glittering, green eyes on Henri. "So be it. If I can't rule, then you will marry my daughter. Take her as your queen. Let your people bow at her feet and do her every bidding."

Henri looks at me, his face ashen.

"If you do not agree," the woman continues, "I will kill this human girl before the magic forces me away—don't think I cannot."

I try to tell Henri not to give in, but the words come out as a nonsensical mumble.

"Fine," the prince bites out. "I agree."

Before I can argue, rail against his decision, or do so much as take a single breath, the troll disappears, taking Henri with her.

I'm left in the still palace, paralyzed by weakness, unable to even cry properly.

Outside the window, the bird continues to sing.

CHAPTER 9

Standing on an old, but well-maintained, wooden porch, I knock on the door in front of me. It's cold in the mountains now. Summer has left, leaving autumn in its place. The cruel wind whips through the valley, clawing at the desperation in my heart.

It took an entire twenty-four hours for my body to heal from the troll's magic. I still ache like I'm recovering from an illness, but I ignore the stiffness in my joints and muscles. I have more important things to focus on.

I'm about to knock again when the woman answers. She gives me a knowing, satisfied smile when she sees me and ushers me inside with a jerk of her head. "Would you like tea, Princess? Perhaps something a bit stronger?"

"Why did you give me the handkerchief the day I met you?" I demand as soon as the door closes behind us. Without waiting for an answer, I continue, "It was because you knew I was staying in the palace. You knew I'd met Henri the night before, didn't you? Don't tell me you didn't because I saw it in your eyes."

I pause as her words catch up with me. "Wait, did you call me 'princess?'"

She laughs, unconcerned by my frazzled appearance or slightly mad behavior. Lowering her shawl, she turns.

Wings.

The old woman in the village has wings.

She's a *fairy*.

"I'll put water on for tea." She turns toward the fire, working efficiently in her tiny one-room cottage. Her wings glitter in the light shining through the open windows. "Sit."

The word is not voiced as a pleasant request; it's a command.

Too overwhelmed to fight her, I plop into the chair and rest my forehead on the table. "I'm surrounded by magic. My family has a fairy godfather, my husband is cursed, my mother-in-law is a troll, and there's a fairy in the village."

The woman makes a tutting sound and places a cup of steaming tea in front of me. She didn't even wait long enough to pretend the water boiled on its own. "Drink."

I eye her. "What will it do to me?"

She sets her hands on her hips and stares at me in a way that has me reaching for the cup. "Not all of us are fools like your Mortimer."

I turn my gaze to the tea. It's been a long time, several months in fact, since I've had a cup. I found leaves in the palace larder, but they were twenty years old. Giving in, I take a sip and almost purr with pleasure.

"You broke the curse," the fairy says, not wasting a moment. "Fell in love with Henri, didn't you? Kissed him and destroyed the troll's malignant magic. It works every time."

Instead of answering, I sputter, trying to find a way to assure her that I'm not in love with Henri. Not really. Not yet.

Surely not.

"And you're here, looking like death, so obviously something went awry." She pushes a sweet biscuit my way. "Tell me."

The entire story pours out. She sits, making understanding noises every so often. Once I'm finished, I lean forward. "I was hoping, since you knew Henri was the bear, that you might be able to tell me how to get to the troll palace Henri spoke of. The palace that's located east of the sun and west of the moon."

She shakes her head and scoots the plate of biscuits toward me when she catches me eying them. "I'm afraid I cannot."

My body sags with disappointment.

"But I can give you this." She rummages through a cupboard and produces a rosy apple. "It will aid you in your quest."

I look at the apple, then at her, and then at the fruit again. I raise an eyebrow. "It's an apple."

"Very good," the woman says, amusement thick in her voice. "A clever girl like you will go far in life."

I accept the gift, wanting very much to roll my eyes. "Thank you." Then I murmur under my breath, "I suppose."

"Saddle my horse and ride along the road, to the east. By evening, you will reach another village. Send the horse home and seek out the woman carding wool on her porch. She lives in the cottage under the cliff."

"How do you know she'll be on her porch?"

"What makes you think she won't?"

I stare at the woman for several moments, wondering if all fairies are mad.

"Fine." It's not like I have any other options.

"Wait," the woman says as I turn to leave. She taps the apple, and to my astonishment, it turns to gold. Not gold like yellow and delicious—actual *gold*. "Now you may leave."

Disconcerted, I stare at the fruit.

"Go on now," the fairy coaxes, hurrying me out.

I look back as I step onto the porch. "I left a cat in the palace. Could you check on her occasionally? Make sure she's alive?"

Rynn will be less than pleased if I let the nuisance die of neglect.

The fairy steps aside and motions to the fire. The scraggly beast lies on a cushion by the hearth, fast-asleep. I would bet this golden apple she wasn't there a moment ago.

Feeling more than a little off-kilter, I nod. "All right then. Thank you."

"Best hurry." The woman hands me a package of biscuits for my travels, gives me an encouraging smile, and closes the door in my face.

I RIDE ALL DAY, and just when I think the woman was

wrong, a village appears in the distance. Once I reach the outskirts of town, I give the tawny buckskin mare a pat, and then I send her back the way we came. She trots off, toward home.

The sun sets behind the nearby, tree-lined cliff, and I wrap Henri's cloak tighter around my shoulders. It carries his forest fragrance and makes my heart ache.

He's only been gone a day, but I miss him.

Why did I kiss him? Why must I always meddle in things I should leave alone?

I walk for twenty-three minutes before I spot the cottage under the cliff. Sure enough, a woman sits on her porch, carding wool.

A familiar woman. Or a familiar fairy, rather.

I walk toward her, frowning. "Hello again."

The fairy I spoke with earlier looks up, smiling. "Do I know you, dear?"

Exasperated, I take another step closer. "We spoke not seven hours ago, in your cottage, near the palace of Briadell."

"I'm afraid I've never ventured near the palace." She leans close, and a smile ghosts across her face as she lowers her voice and says, "Have you heard? Our prince is cursed."

My eye twitches.

Fine. I'll play her game.

"I'm looking for a palace in Elsland that's said to be east of the sun and west of the moon. Can you tell me how to get there?"

"I cannot." She sets her wool aside, disrupting a sleeping cat in her basket.

My jaw drops as Rynn's beast stretches and looks up at me, yawning with disinterest.

"But I can give you this to aid in your journey." The woman holds out the tool she was using.

I purse my lips as I look back at the fairy, trying to contain my irritation. After I trust myself to speak in a civil tone, I ask, "Your carding comb? Do you think that will be of help to me?"

The fairy nods solemnly. "Most assuredly. Now, you must travel eight hours to the east. There's a woman who can help you in the next village. Look for her in a cottage by the waterfall. She'll be spinning wool on her porch."

"It will be the middle of the night when I reach her, and yet you say she'll be on her porch, spinning wool?"

Instead of answering, the woman adds, "You may ride my horse, but remember to send her home as soon as you reach the village."

Unable to help myself, I let out a small, mirthless laugh. "That's very kind of you."

"You are most welcome," she says graciously and leads me toward the barn.

I follow her but stop as soon as I pass the doors. The buckskin mare stares at me as she chews a clump of hay.

Turning back to the fairy, I demand, "Now that's enough. What game are we playing?"

The woman gives me an innocent look. "I don't understand."

"That's the horse I rode here!"

She shakes her head. "No. She's been in my barn all this time."

A headache blooms at the base of my skull, but I give the fairy a curt nod. "Fine. Thank you."

She watches as I saddle the horse, but before I leave, she calls me back. Without so much as asking permission, she pulls the carding comb from the satchel I wear. With a quick tap, it turns to gold.

"Now you may leave."

Shaking my head, I take the road east. The horse trots at a comfortable pace, apparently unconcerned that she walked all day. We reach the village by the waterfall exactly eight hours later, in the middle of the night, and I send the horse home. She gives me a friendly nicker and then ambles back the way we came.

I watch the mare with suspicious eyes, waiting for her to double back. Eventually, I give up and turn toward the village.

I'm not the least bit surprised when I find the *very same fairy* sitting on her porch, working with the tiniest spinning wheel I've ever seen.

She looks up when she spots me, and her eyes spark with humor. "Pleasant night, isn't it?"

It's frigid actually.

I force a smile. "I am looking for a palace in Elsland. It's said to be located east of the sun and west of the moon. Can you tell me the way?"

When I step forward, I startle the cat that's fast asleep on her lap. The feline turns my way, peering at me with her familiar yellow stare, almost as if she's in on the ruse.

"There is no road, I'm afraid," the fairy says, drawing my attention from the cat.

"Then how do I travel there?"

She shrugs. "The wind may take you if you can convince him your quest is a noble one."

I shift, thankful for a change of answer. "It is. But how do I speak with the *wind?*"

"He's a fairy, child. As substantial as you or me."

"*Another* fairy?" I say, losing my patience.

The woman ignores my tone. "Take my horse and my spinning wheel. Ride to the east. He lives on the highest peak in Briadell."

Gently setting Rynn's cat aside, the woman leads me to a familiar buckskin mare. The horse whinnies in greeting, happy to see me again. I don't bother to mention it to the fairy.

"Good luck to you," the woman says as I lead the horse outside.

"Aren't you forgetting something?" I hold out the miniature spinning wheel.

The fairy's eyes sparkle. "Oh, yes."

With a tap of her finger, the spinning wheel turns to gold.

"Take care with the wind fairies," she warns as I mount the horse. "They tend to make a habit of sending people on wild goose chases."

I take a moment to rein in my agitation, and then I thank her for her help.

Once again, I'm riding east, toward the sunrise, toward the East Wind, and hopefully, toward Henri.

CHAPTER 10

The house is the loneliest I've ever seen, built on the top of a windy peak. Its only company is a family of several boulders of various sizes, all covered in sage-green moss. The trees are far below. Even they don't want to grow this close to the sky.

My horse is exhausted. We've traveled for a full week, resting sporadically along the way. I practically fall from the saddle.

Immediately, she turns around and heads for home.

"You're just going to leave me?" I call to the mare.

She angles back, gives me an equine look of disinterest, and continues on her way.

Sighing, I turn back to the house. It doesn't look as if anyone has lived here for years. It's no great surprise when no one answers the door.

Now what do I do?

I could run after the horse, attempt to find another desolate peak. Or I could go inside, light a fire, and wallow in despair. Though the last option has its appeal, it wouldn't solve much.

I suppose I could call Mortimer, but he doesn't answer me now—hasn't since he said he was done with me. Some fairy godfather.

Just as I'm mulling over my options, the air shimmers and sparks, and there materializes a tall man with a snowy beard, alarmingly bushy eyebrows, and a long, thin nose.

Startled by his abrupt appearance, I stumble into the closed door.

Even more startled by *me*, the fairy steps back, trips on a rock, and falls on his posterior with an, "Ooof!"

I rush forward, extending my hand. "I'm so sorry," I say, realizing I've possibly ruined my only chance to find the troll palace. He'll never help me now. If I know anything about fairies, it's that they don't care for human girls who make them look foolish.

While pulling the wind fairy to his feet, I murmur countless apologies.

He brushes himself off, frowning, and then finally peers at me with such concentration, his huge eyebrows meet. "Who are you?"

"I'm Sophia of Astoria—actually, I suppose I'm Sophia of Briadell now. I'm looking for my husband, who has been taken by the troll queen. I was told you'd know how to find a palace in Elsland that's located east of the sun and west of the moon."

The man takes a moment to digest the information, and then he slowly nods. "I've heard of it, but I don't know the way. Perhaps my brother, the West Wind—"

"No. Absolutely not." I take a step forward. "I've already played this game. First, you'll send me to the West Wind, and then he'll send me to the North. The North Wind will send me to the South, and then finally, when I am old and gray, and my husband is celebrating his golden anniversary with his troll bride, I'll arrive at the palace!"

One bushy eyebrow raises as I finish my spiel. "Are you quite finished?"

Feeling a bit foolish for the outburst, I nod.

"I believe the West Wind would have sent you to the South Wind, not the North."

I resist the urge to throttle him—because he's both my elder and a fairy, and it won't do Henri any good if the East Wind turns me into a mountain goat.

"Please, *please*," I beg, "take me to Elsland yourself."

The fairy gives me a wry smile. "Very well. I'll see if I can find the way."

BY THE TIME I tumble to the ground, my face is numb from the chill of the wind, my body aches, and after a quick inspection, I find my hair feels like a rat made its home in my once-smooth tresses.

Next to me, the East Wind wheezes and stumbles forward, barely keeping his balance.

I rub my cheeks, trying to work feeling back into them, and look around, taking in my new surroundings.

So, this is Elsland.

We're in the high mountains, and the nearby snow-covered cliffs are golden in the late afternoon light. Jagged, indigo peaks rise in the far distance, cutting into the horizon.

Below us, in a nearby valley, tall, statuesque pines grow. Their boughs are dusted with snow, and the deciduous trees have already lost their leaves for the year. Just across the valley, on the tallest nearby peak, sits a cold, lonely palace. It's taller than it is wide, built of gray stone, and the turrets are roofed in dusky blue.

"From here, you walk," the East Wind groans.

"Is that it?" I ask, motioning to the castle. "The palace?"

The fairy nods and raises his hands. With a strong gust of wind that kicks up the snow at my feet, he's gone.

I shiver under Henri's cloak as I look at the palace. I'm here, but what do I do now? It's not as if I can walk to the door and demand the troll woman gives me Henri back. And it will be dark soon.

Without a clear plan in mind, I walk toward the palace. The snow grows deeper as I drop into the valley, and I sink into it with every step I take. It tops my boots and slides down my leg.

Frozen, I pull the fleece-lined hood over my head, wishing I'd thought to bring a change of clothing with me. The sun sinks lower. No matter how far I walk, the forest never recedes.

The sun sets behind the distant mountains, and twilight shadows the path. Massive pines tower on either side of my trail, making it impossible to see the palace in the distance.

Left with no choice, I continue. Just before the last of

the sun's light fades from the landscape, I hear the far-off tinkling of bells.

The sound steadily grows until its source is right behind me. Two snowy horses trot into view, pulling a sleigh. Tiny silver bells line their harnesses, and they jingle with the horses' every movement, letting off a cheerful, welcome sound. Perhaps it's for that reason, in a split-second decision that could quite possibly cost me my life, I leap in front of the horses and hold out my arms.

The animals shy back, coming to an abrupt halt that jars the sleigh and its passengers.

"Why have we stopped?" a loud, female voice asks.

I lower my arms, stepping back, realizing my mistake too late. That voice—

"Well, what is it?" the woman says, standing in the sleigh to see around her driver.

Surreptitiously, I tug the front of my hood lower, hoping to cast my face in shadows.

A pretty face comes into view, framed with a cascade of perfect ringlets. The woman is not Henri's stepmother as I feared when I first heard her speak, though she looks and sounds very much like her. Except there is amusement in her voice, perhaps even a kindness that is at odds with her kind.

"Why are you standing in the road, little troll?"

Little troll? She thinks I'm a child? And one of *them?* I look down at the way Henri's cloak pools in the snow at my feet, and then I turn my attention to the statuesque, beautiful troll addressing me.

Clearing my throat, I take a cautious step forward. "I'm on my way to the palace."

"Brave one, aren't you?" She eyes me with good humor. She's not old, most likely Rynn's age. "Aren't you afraid of Queen Amara? She is quite fearsome."

"I have a wedding gift for Her Highness," I say, producing the golden apple. Even in the dim light, it shines.

"Oh, I rather like that," the pretty troll says, leaning forward to better see the fruit. "A wedding gift for Ambrosia, you say?"

I nod.

She thinks about it for a moment, and then she asks, "How much will you take for it?"

"It's not for sale," I answer, hoping I can wrangle a ride to the palace. "Not for gold…"

The troll laughs, delighted. Her voice is as delicate as the bells her horses wear. "Fair enough. What will you trade it for?"

"A ride to the palace."

After a moment, she motions me over. "You should have asked for more, little troll. I wasn't going to leave you to freeze."

I trudge through the snow to meet her, terrified she's going to realize I'm neither child nor troll. The driver leaps from his seat and offers me a hand into the carriage. Just as I'm about to take it, I freeze.

There, sitting on the plush seat next to the beautiful troll, is Henri. His eyes are intent in the near-dark, and they drill into mine, conveying a hundred emotions. He finally settles on irritation.

This isn't part of his plan. It's hard to sacrifice himself, all in the name of saving my life, if I chase after him and put myself in harm's way.

But just seeing Henri makes my heart clench, and I choke back a relieved sob. Let him be angry with me—I don't care. I've found him.

"Oh, little one," the troll gasps as soon as I step into the sleigh. "You reek of fairy magic."

Hovering awkwardly, not daring to sit, I look at my feet.

"And something else." Curiosity lights her eyes, and she shifts forward. Before I can stop her, she pushes back my hood. "Human."

She doesn't say it with disgust or contempt. It's more the way someone would comment on a creature darting across a field: *Look there—it's a fox.* Or a deer, squirrel, badger or…

"Human," she says again, shaking her head and making soft chastising noises. "That's not good."

She glances at Henri, grinning in a coquettish way. "You people are like mice. Let one in, and suddenly the whole kingdom's infested."

And suddenly, ridiculous though it may be, jealousy washes over me. Who is this woman—this *troll*—who dares flirt with my husband?

Unfortunately, I've never been good at concealing my emotions, and the woman's eyes sparkle in the near-dark of the twilight forest. "Tell me, little human, are you acquainted with my dear stepbrother, Prince Henri of Briadell?"

"She's no one," Henri says caustically, making me glare at him. "Just a foolish acquaintance with grand ideas. If you have magic enough, send her back to the capital city of Astoria."

The words hurt, but I'm not a fool. I know what he's doing, but before I can argue with him, the situation dawns on me. The girl is Henri's stepsister, the troll queen's daughter...the woman—and I'm using that term loosely—he's supposed to marry.

"You're Ambrosia," I say, my voice slightly more accusatory than I intend. "The troll princess."

"Around here, we usually drop the troll bit. It's rather unnecessary, don't you think?" She flashes Henri another look. "Or it was before you humans started to pop up."

"Send her home." Henri's voice is strong, but there's a plea in there, one his betrothed notices.

She angles her head toward him and then looks at me. After a moment, her quizzical frown turns into a radiant smile. "You're her—Henri's human wife. The one who foolishly went and fell in love with him and broke the fairy-addled curse." She grins at Henri, whose face is now like stone. "And she followed you here? Isn't that remarkably sweet?"

I swallow, fighting back my embarrassment. She makes it sound so ridiculous. Like I've been nothing more than a pawn all along, and I've overstepped my part in the game.

"Give me the apple," Ambrosia says, holding out her palm. "I'll take you to the palace and sneak you into Henri's room tonight."

I stare at her, my mouth partially agape.

"Come on now." She wiggles her fingers, demanding her payment.

"Why would you do that?"

She arches a single eyebrow in a move so perfectly executed, I want to learn it myself. "I don't want him. Do I look like the sort of troll who must resort to marrying a human?"

Unsure how to answer, I give her a wobbly shake of my head. "No?"

"No," she parrots sternly. "I have more than ten suitors, and I do not intend to give them up for one of my mother's whims. Henri is entertaining, no doubt, but you are welcome to him."

"What about your mother?" I demand.

Ambrosia clasps her hands together, making her ringlets dance, and sighs with great contentment. "She will be livid when she finds out you've come for him."

Slowly, my unease lessens, and I drop into the seat opposite Ambrosia and Henri. Though unlikely, I believe I've found a troll after my own heart.

The princess coos over the apple for several moments, and then she tells the driver to continue. I glance at Henri, wondering what he makes of the situation, but he stares ahead, his face expressionless.

CHAPTER 11

Ambrosia's even lovelier in the light of the castle, though I immediately spot her tell. Her nose is turned up at the very end, almost as if she's trying to conceal a great, long snout with her magic.

She flounces around Henri's room, telling me exactly when to expect him back again this evening. When she catches me studying her, the princess covers her face with her hand. "It's awful, isn't it?"

"No…" I cringe as I slowly say the word.

With a loud groan, she flops her tall, willowy frame into a nearby chair. "Don't bother lying. We have mirrors after all—I can see it. No matter how I try, I can't conceal it."

"I didn't notice in the woods." This time, it's the truth.

"Yes, I suppose it could be worse," she admits with a lazy shrug.

She sits there for so long, I begin to wonder if she's going to leave. Henri's already in the dining hall, playing dutiful house guest—and all to protect me. It's not that surprising he's angry I'm here.

I'm afraid he'll have to get over it.

"I should go," Ambrosia says after several long minutes.

As she stands, I open my mouth only to close it again.

"Spit it out," she says, catching me.

"You're not what I expected," I admit.

Her eyes light with amusement. "Not all trolls are like my mother."

"Are most of them?"

After all, I'd like to know what I'm up against.

"Yes, most are." She grins at me as she opens the door behind her. "Best not answer the door. In fact, hide under the bed."

"For how long?" I ask, aghast.

"Only until Henri returns."

"And how long will that—"

I'm answered by the slamming door.

I look around the room, wondering if there is somewhere else I could hide. Left with no other option, I scoot under the bed.

Ten o'clock goes by and then eleven. Somewhere before midnight, I doze off.

The door swings open and voices sound in the room. I wake with such a start, I knock my head on the frame and have to bite my tongue to keep from crying out.

With every one of my muscles tensed and ready to flee, I listen to the brief conversation Henri has with his stepmother.

"You must convince her," the troll queen insists when

Henri points out Ambrosia has refused to marry him every night he's asked for her hand.

"If you cannot, I promise the human girl you left in Briadell will suffer for your lack of perseverance."

With that, the door closes. Still, I don't dare move.

After several long moments, Henri whispers, "Sophie?"

Relieved, I crawl on my belly, scooting from under the bed like a weasel. Before I can find my feet, Henri pulls me into his arms and holds me tightly. "You are a foolish, foolish girl," he whispers into my hair. "How did you find me?"

I tell him of the fairies, and though my tale isn't long, by the end, he's yawning.

"I'm sorry." I gently poke him in the side, chastising him with a teasing scowl. "Am I boring you with the details?"

He shakes his head, but he fights a yawn yet again. "She must have drugged me at dinner."

That's inconvenient.

"What will we do?" For the first time, I hear the fear in my voice. We need to escape.

We need to escape *tonight*.

Henri pulls me to the bed, unable to keep his eyes open. "We'll discuss it in the morning."

I burrow close to him, but I don't dare sleep. I jump at every noise—every creak, every gust of wind outside the tall, slender windows.

Near morning, I try to wake Henri, but it's an impossible task. The troll queen's magic is too potent.

Just after dawn, as I'm lying on my side, staring at

Henri, *willing* him to wake, I hear footsteps outside the door.

I leap from the bed, looking for a place to dart as the door swings open.

Ambrosia stands on the other side, key in hand, shaking her head. "Now what would you have done if I'd been my mother?"

"You didn't tell me the queen would give him a sleeping draught!" I hiss as I fight back my fright.

The pretty troll shrugs. "You didn't ask."

Wrinkling my nose, I stare at her.

Ambrosia's response sounds an awful lot like something *I* would say. No wonder Father's always so irritated with me.

"Well, you didn't." She laughs at the sour look on my face. "And now you have to leave because Mother will be along any minute."

And that's when I hear it—the ominous sound of the troll queen screeching at a servant down the hall.

"Where should I go?" I demand.

Ambrosia shrugs again. "Out the window?"

"We're in a tower!"

"Therefore, I suggest you watch your step."

Even though there is no time to waste, I gawk at her, certain she must be joking. When she makes a "scoot along" gesture with her hand, I realize she's not.

Growling under my breath, I hurry to the window and toss the dappled glass open. Then I look over my shoulder, glaring at the troll princess. "There's a balcony just under us."

"Of course there is. What did you think? That I'd

expect you to sprout wings?" She grins and gives me a shove.

I cast Henri one last rueful look, and then I crawl out the window, down to the safety of the terrace below. The morning wind is bitter from traveling the nearby icy peaks, and it bites at my hands and face.

Shivering, I drop to the balcony and realize I left Henri's cloak in the room. Just as my feet touch the frosted stones, Ambrosia pokes her head out the window. "Watch for the snow griffins. They roost this time of year, and they're not particularly friendly."

"What are—"

The princess closes the window, cutting off my question.

Why do people keep doing that to me?

Frustrated, I rub my hands over my crossed arms for warmth and scan the turrets, looking for signs of the griffins Ambrosia spoke of. There's a stray gray feather on the stone rail that could be from a griffin—or most likely a pigeon—but I don't catch a single glimpse of the beasts themselves.

Sunlight, warm and welcoming, crests the eastern peaks. It shines down on the wooded valley, stretching all the way into the distance, chasing away the night. I angle my face toward it, grateful it's a cloudless morning.

After several minutes, I look around. No stairs lead to the balcony, and the tower is built of smooth, slick stones that would be impossible to climb. Glancing behind me, I frown. There's a door, one I most likely don't want to enter. Looking up, I try to decide if I could crawl back to Henri's window in a while.

Alas, it's a little too high.

Left with no choice, I try the door. As I feared, it's locked. I'm trapped here, waiting for Henri or Ambrosia to rescue me. Of course, Henri doesn't know where I'm at, so I suppose I must rely on the kindness of the troll princess.

Once the sun melts the frost, I sit with my back against the wall and look out over the forest. Steam rises from a nearby river. It's half-covered in ice, beautiful, and serene.

As harsh as it is, Elsland is breathtaking. If the trolls didn't guard it so tenaciously, surely a human king would claim it for his own. I draw my legs to my chest in a feeble attempt to keep warm and take in the scenery, all the while planning an escape that is looking less likely by the minute.

I'm fortunate I got here at all. What did I expect? That I'd show up undetected and spirit Henri away?

"Little human?" a now-familiar voice calls from Henri's room. "Still down there?"

Not bothering to stand, I crane my head up to look at Ambrosia. "There are no stairs, and the door is locked. Where did you expect me to go?"

"Hmmm."

That all she says. *Hmmm.*

"Do you think you could unlock the door?" I ask, my frozen fingers and toes making me lose my patience.

She sets her elbow on the ledge, drops her chin in her palm, and nods. The motion makes the sun catch her perfectly-spiraled ringlets. "I could."

I wait a moment.

"Will you, please?" I say once I realize she's not going to make this easy.

Five minutes and twenty-seven seconds later, Ambrosia opens the door.

"Where's Henri?" I demand as soon as I walk over the threshold.

"I have an errand," Ambrosia says absently, ignoring my question as she leads me through what appears to be a seldom-used sitting room. The drapes are pulled, and the room is quite dark and depressing. "You'll come with me."

Stopping by a linen-covered chair, I set my hands on my hips. "You think so, do you?"

The pretty troll looks over her shoulder. "Do you have something better to do? I'm not sure you want to wander around the palace. Most of us have lost our taste for humans, but the elders still remember the glorious days of old." She leans close, her eyes bright, and says conspiratorially, "Rumor has it you taste like chickens."

I cringe. "You're bluffing."

Ambrosia shrugs. "Your choice."

And then she walks through the door, into the hall. I tap my finger on my hip, frowning.

Trolls don't eat humans. They curse us, blight us, set our villages ablaze. But they don't *eat* us.

Do they?

Another few seconds go by.

"Ambrosia!" I hurry through the room, scurrying after the troll princess.

CHAPTER 12

"What are we doing?" I demand as we go deeper and deeper into the depths of the palace. "Where are we going?"

The walls, which up higher were made of smooth, rectangular stones, have morphed into mismatched, flat rocks of all shapes and sizes. I haven't seen a window in almost ten minutes, and though we haven't passed a single fire, the cool air seems to stay a constant temperature.

I'm not sure how far underground we are, but I'm quite confident we're not in the palace anymore.

Instead of answering my question, Ambrosia launches into a dry speech about Elsland's grand history. Even she sounds bored, so I know she's just evading my questions.

Fifteen minutes later, the air begins to warm, and it grows steadily hotter as we continue down the passage.

Again, I ask, "Where are we going?"

"Here," she says as the narrow hallway ends at a series of five steps that lead up to a door. It's a massive thing, with iron braces and a heavy lock. The chamber ahead looks ominous, like the kind of place a troll would take a human to torture her.

Without hesitation, Ambrosia tosses the door open, and we're hit with a curtain of hot air.

A forge burns in the middle of the room, and flames dance over red-hot coals like a living creature.

Apparently, it's less a torture chamber and more a smithy. A chimney tops the forge, and it disappears into the rock above, taking smoke with it.

"Johan!" Ambrosia calls as she saunters into the room.

And that's when I see him. The troll. The troll who looks like a troll.

The troll who's…not that bad, actually.

He looks up, probably as startled to see me as I am to see him. His eyes are a smidgen too close together, and his shoulders are slightly hunched. His skin is smudged with soot, but to my great surprise, it's not green as I'd always been told.

"New pet?" he asks the princess, looking leery.

"She's cute, isn't she?" Ambrosia bops me on the head in a patronizing fashion. "I'm thinking of keeping her. She's a tame little thing—hasn't made a fuss. It will all depend on how much she eats."

The troll at the forge grunts. I glare at Ambrosia, but she only smirks and produces the golden apple from the folds of her gown. With a flick of her wrist, she tosses it to the smith.

With surprisingly quick reflexes, he catches the apple with ease. He narrows his eyes, studying the golden fruit, turning it over in his palm before he throws it back. "It's tainted."

Ambrosia catches the apple mid-air and scowls. "It's *gold*."

"It's fairy gold," he says, practically spitting the word.

Apparently, there's no love lost between the two races.

The princess points to her nose. "Do you see this? It's larger than yesterday. I need you to melt down the apple!"

Shaking his head, the smith refuses. "Too dangerous."

"You can do it."

"The timing is impossible."

"Johan, it's not a request." Apple in her palm, Ambrosia sets her hands on her hips.

After several long seconds, Johan meets her eyes. "Fine," he says, perhaps not daring to defy his princess. "But if we go even a moment too long, the forge will explode. You best send your pet out."

I ignore the pet remark and step forward. "How long is too long?"

Johan watches me for a moment, perhaps trying to decide if he's going to answer a human. "I have four minutes to extract the lingering fairy magic from the gold—and not a second more. If I go over, my magic will merge with the fairy's, and the results will be catastrophic."

A slow frown builds on Ambrosia's face. "Johan's probably right," she finally says.

The smith begins to nod, glad Ambrosia has come to her senses and realized she should leave well enough alone.

"You should probably leave before we begin," she finishes, looking at me.

Johan's face falls.

I turn to the princess, standing my ground even as she attempts to shove me toward the door. "If I help you, will you let me see Henri tonight?"

"Help?" She laughs like I've said something truly amusing. "What could you possibly do?"

I've never been proud of my gift. In fact, I tell as few people as possible. But right now, I'm grateful for it.

"Every moment of the day, I know exactly what time it is; therefore, I know—down to the second—how much time has elapsed. I can tell Johan the very moment he must finish his task."

Ambrosia narrows her eyes, studying me. "That's a strange gift for a fairy godmother to bestow."

I wrinkle my nose. "My family ended up with a fairy godfather."

She looks momentarily perplexed, and then she nods. "Fine then. Stay here, help if you can. But I simply cannot be held responsible if you die a horrible, fiery, *excruciating* death. Is that clear?"

I gulp but find it in myself to nod. "And Henri?"

Sighing, she says, "I don't know. I've grown rather tired of the game. It was amusing at first, but I have no desire to make a habit of sneaking you about the palace."

Without hesitation, I pull the golden carding comb from the deep pocket stitched in my gown.

The lovely troll's eyes go wide, and she immediately reaches for the comb.

Making a tsking noise, I pull it back.

"All right," she says, her greedy eyes still on the comb. "I'll sneak you in again."

Nodding, I hand her the comb. "And you'll keep your mother from slipping Henri the sleeping draught?"

The princess gives the comb a loving stroke and says in a chiding voice, "You should have asked that *before* you handed me the comb."

I give her a disbelieving look, but she only smiles.

Do I dare trade away the spinning wheel? It's the only thing I have left.

But what choice do I have? It won't do me a bit of good if Henri falls dead asleep again tonight.

Making up my mind, I pull out the tiny spinning wheel.

Ambrosia gasps. "Just how much are you hiding in your skirts?"

"I can hold her upside down and give her a good shake," Johan offers ever so helpfully.

Taking a cautious step away from the smith, I clasp the spinning wheel to my chest. "This is the last of it."

And the princess wants it. With her eyes trained on the golden tool, she nibbles her lip.

"Promise me you'll prevent your mother from giving Henri the sleeping draught tonight," I demand.

Her expression flickers with indecision. Then, rolling her eyes as if she thinks I'm a bore, she finally agrees. "Yes, all right. Now give me the spinning wheel."

She holds her hands out like a greedy toddler.

Nervous I used my gifts foolishly, I give her the spinning wheel. Once it's in her hands, she clutches it, the apple, and the comb to her chest, holding them like they are precious.

"I'll be beautiful for at least a year with this much

gold," she says, her voice thick with gluttonous satisfaction.

Johan mutters to himself as he prepares the fire, and I cross my arms. "What does the gold do?"

Ambrosia rubs the comb against her cheek. "In its molten form, we are able to use it as an amplifier for our magic."

"Once we strip the fairy magic," Johan gripes to himself as he stokes the fire.

The hot room becomes sweltering, and I wipe my brow with the back of my hand. Johan collects the golden items from Ambrosia, and then, using only his hands, breaks them into small pieces.

I watch him, vaguely disconcerted. Gold's soft. But still.

Sweat rolls down his forehead as he melts the gold. Once it's in its molten state, he says, "Begin the time now. We have four minutes—not a second over."

Then he begins the arduous task of pulling the fairy magic from the metal. His arm muscles bulge, and his jaw is clenched so tightly, a vein throbs in his forehead.

My task is as simple as breathing. I merely watch, waiting.

Johan growls several times as he works the metal. At first, the gold turns green, and then it shifts to a silver color as the troll magic fights the fairy's. Excluding the time Henri's troll-mother had me writhing in pain, I've never witnessed their magic. I don't know if it's because the task in front of him is particularly difficult, or if troll magic is simply crude in nature, but it looks far more taxing than the fairy magic I've seen all my life.

"Fifteen seconds," I warn, growing slightly nervous. "Fourteen."

The smith growls as he fights with the silver, viscous liquid.

"Five, four, three—" I glance at the door, wondering if I should have left when I had the chance. "Two..."

Before my eyes, the metal returns to its expected golden color, and Johan steps back, filtering a purple, minuscule cloud of magic into a pewter vial by his side. He corks the top and lets out a long sigh.

"Well?" Ambrosia prods, eager to hear whether Johan was able to remove all the magic.

Personally, I consider the fact that there was no explosion a success.

Johan nods and waves a sooty hand to the molten gold. "Go on then."

With a girly squeal that shouldn't leave a grown woman—much less a grown troll, Ambrosia leaps forward and extends her hands, sending her magic into the metal once more. This time, instead of turning silver, it glows white like a diamond. She bounces on the balls of her feet as she works. When it looks like she might be coming to a finish, Johan uncorks another pewter bottle, this one scrolled and lovely, and holds it for her as she sends the diamond-colored magic into it.

With a satisfied grin, Ambrosia casts the remnants of the enchantment over her body. She glows for several seconds, and then the magic fades.

"Well?" she asks, turning her head so I can see her profile. "Is it smaller?"

Her nose is perfectly pert, quite human, and as pretty as a nose can be. Still, it's a lot of fuss for a troll snout.

I nod, and she clasps the newly filled vial to her chest. "Oh, how marvelous!"

More interested in the cooling gold than the princess and her nose, I stare at the metal. It still hasn't returned to its golden color. It's white, and it shimmers in the light. Quite beautiful.

"What do you do with it now?" I ask. "Can you use it again?"

Johan takes a pair of iron tongs, picks up the entire pot, and tosses it in a bucket of water. The hot gold hisses when it makes contact with the liquid, and an angry cloud of steam rises. After it cools, he pulls out the hardened metal blob and tosses it into the corner of the room as if it's nothing more than scrap metal.

I didn't notice the pile of discarded precious metal before, but now I gape at it. The rounded, uneven lumps look nothing like they did in their previous state—nothing like gold at all. Indeed, they look like they were made from pearls, if pearls were somehow transformed into a meltable, maleable metal.

The troll gives me a grim smile when he catches me staring. "It takes a good deal of gold to keep Her Highness looking beautiful."

Ambrosia, in a move that finally convinces me there's a troll underneath that lovely exterior, cuffs the side of his head.

Johan winces, rubbing his ear. As the two bicker, I have an epiphany.

"Your mother wants Briadell for its gold," I say out loud.

The princess looks over. "Well, of course. Why else would we want it? I hate to break it to you, since you're probably fond of the little kingdom, but it's infested with humans."

Ignoring her, I point to the pile. "Is it worthless now that you've used it?"

Ambrosia sighs, realizing I don't intend to move on. "It can't be used twice, if that's what you're asking."

"I mean, it's still gold, isn't it?" Gingerly, I walk to the pile and pick up one of the opalescent blobs. It's cool to the touch, a bit cumbersome, and warms in my hand.

"I suppose." She doesn't look terribly interested.

"What do you do with it?"

Ambrosia shares a look with Johan, as if she's thinking her pet human is a bit daft. "We toss it out. It's no use to us now."

"It's beautiful. Have you ever tried to craft anything out of it?"

Johan scoffs, but Ambrosia steps forward, her eyes narrowed.

I offer her the metal, hoping she'll take a closer look. "If you can work this, people will buy it. If you have smiths willing to experiment with crafting, you could sell it and purchase all the regular gold you want."

And not try to steal my husband's kingdom.

"Do you think so?" the princess asks, though she sounds skeptical.

Johan shakes his head, dismissing the idea, and grunts, "Who would do business with a troll?"

"Briadell will," I immediately offer, knowing Henri likely won't be pleased I'm making business ventures in his stead. "Free Henri, let us go, leave Briadell be, and we will trade with you. In fact, we'll buy all that discarded gold in your pile there—a pound of gold for a pound of your pearl-gold creation."

It's a lot of money—more than I've ever seen in my life, but Briadell is known for its mines. Surely Henri won't mind me buying his freedom.

Well, he might, but I'll deal with that later.

Ambrosia purses her lips, thinking. Finally, she says, "Pound for pound?"

I nod.

"Fine. You have one night to convince Henri." A radiant smile spreads over her face, her eyes already dreamy at the thought of all the gold I'm offering her. Then her tone cools as she meets my eyes. "If he agrees, I will deal with Mother."

Despite the heat of the forge, I shiver at the ominous tone of Ambrosia's promise.

CHAPTER 13

I lie under Henri's bed for the second time, waiting for him to return. Ten minutes after midnight, the door opens. I tense, waiting.

"Sophie?" Henri calls, his voice far more confident than yesterday.

I crawl from under the bed. He waits for me this time, his expression light. Halfway out, I freeze when I spot him. His arms are crossed loosely over his chest, and he leans against the door in a relaxed manner. He seems freer than last night, far less panicked.

Without my permission, my eyes wander over him, taking him in. Even here, in this grand palace, he continues to dress like a warrior prince, wearing a dark brown jerkin made of smooth, supple leather. His trousers are a shade darker than the jerkin, but his shirt is cream and fine.

Oddly, his hair remains white-blond, and it's a striking contrast against his tanned skin. I assumed it was a product of the curse, but it's either the color he was born with or hints of magic linger. He wears it back, in a short tail at his neck.

He cleans up very nicely, this husband of mine.

"I understand you bought a cartload of scrap gold from Ambrosia." Henri says the words brusquely, but there's humor in his eyes.

I shimmy the rest of the way from under the bed and pull myself to my feet. "Ambrosia told you about that, did she?"

"And you didn't think you should perhaps ask my permission first?" He pushes away from the wall, walking toward me.

Gulping, I take a step back—and not because I'm afraid of him. No, I'm afraid of *myself*, of the fluttering in my stomach and the way my heart races when he looks at me as he is now. I skirt the bed and finally bump into a wardrobe.

"I rather assumed it was my place as your wife to care for Briadell in your absence," I explain. "And what better way to care for it than bring you home?"

Henri closes the distance between us. He's so tall, my gaze is level with his chest.

"I see." He leans down until we are face to face. His eyes light with humor, but that doesn't help the situation. My hands itch to move along his arms, his neck, his chest. I clench them into fists at my sides.

His palms find the sides of my hips, and I bite back a soft exclamation. He shifts even closer.

The nearness is enough to make my mouth go dry, and my eyes travel to the topmost buckle of his jerkin. Unable to help myself, I lean toward him and breathe in the woodland scent he carries.

It's a heady fragrance, and it makes my knees soft. If that's a product of his curse, then, by all means, he may turn back into the bear occasionally.

"I think it's acceptable if my queen makes a few business transactions of her own," he murmurs.

My eyes fly to his. His queen?

Princess, yes—all right. But queen? Heaven help Briadell.

"You're not upset?" I ask.

"No." Henri shakes his head. "But Ambrosia must still convince her mother."

I nod as if I'm paying attention to the conversation, but I'm not. My whole being is focused on the heat of Henri's hands. On the way he towers over me, making me feel small but so very *safe*. He's saying something else—something about the troll queen, but I couldn't care less at the moment.

"Henri?" I interrupt.

"Hmmm?"

"We're finally alone, you're no longer a bear, and you aren't asleep on your feet, yet we're talking about your awful stepmother. *Why?*" I ask, my voice tinged with irritation and need. "Am I allowed to ask you to kiss me now? Is that what you're waiting for?"

He goes still. Finally, with his voice a shade darker, he says, "You didn't wait for permission the first time."

I move closer. "I don't make a habit of asking for permission *ever*."

"Then why bother now?"

Growing exasperated, I shift closer. "Because I—"

Without letting me finish the sentence, Henri tugs me flush against him. He pauses briefly, almost as if he's prolonging the moment, and then, just when I think I will surely die if he doesn't follow through, his lips claim mine.

I let out a sound of surprise, and he smiles before he deepens the kiss. I lean into him, wishing I'd broken the awful curse sooner.

He cradles the back of my neck and twines his fingers through my hair. My hands travel his chest and eventually hang with my arms draped over his shoulders. I lean against him, temporarily unable to stand on my wobbly legs.

When Henri pulls back, my brain is delightfully fuzzy.

"Better?" he asks, his voice still husky.

I give him a mischievous smile. "And here I thought you were avoiding it because you were so dreadfully out of practice."

He growls under his breath, laughing darkly, and moves to kiss me again as if to prove, once and for all, he wasn't staying away from me due to his lack of prowess.

Just as our lips barely touch the second time, Henri's door swings open with a bang.

Queen Amara stands in the doorway, looking livid. Ambrosia's with her, though the princess doesn't appear to be as concerned as I feel she should be.

The troll queen fixes her eyes on Henri. "You are a fool, even for a human. Why would you want *her* when you could have my daughter?"

Ambrosia begins to speak only to have her mother jerk

a hand up, demanding silence. The princess closes her mouth and rolls her eyes. She seems calm, but I'm a rabbit ready to dart. Fear courses through my veins, making my already lightheaded-self dizzy.

It took me a full twenty-four hours to recover from my first meeting with the troll queen. My muscles ache at the memory of her magic.

Henri nudges me behind him. "Your own daughter agreed to the bargain."

The troll queen points at me, and I shy back. "There isn't one thing that pathetic, scrawny human can do that my daughter cannot do better. Ambrosia is beautiful, poised, witty—she's everything you could possibly want in a bride."

"Except I'm a troll," Ambrosia says wryly, earning another nasty look from her mother. "He doesn't seem to care for that."

"What if I give Ambrosia a task," Henri says abruptly, startling the queen and the princess both.

"A task?" Amara asks, narrowing her eyes.

Henri nods, growing confident. "That's right—a test if you will. Whichever girl can complete it will be my wife. If Ambrosia wins, I won't fight you any longer. If Sophie wins, then you leave us and my kingdom be."

The queen looks understandably suspicious. "Why would you do that? Why offer a test when that human girl has already made a bargain for your freedom?"

"I know you'll never let us go, not unless it's your choice. And I would rather marry Ambrosia than watch you hurt Sophie again." Henri turns to me slowly, waiting until our gazes meet. "I love her."

Warmth spreads over me, making me feel as if I'm in a meadow in the dead of summer and not in this cold, lonely palace.

Henri loves me.

"Fine," Amara says, sounding disgusted as she flips her long black hair over her shoulder. "But there is no test you can give my daughter that she won't excel at."

Henri flashes me a grin.

"There might be one." He begins to unlace his fine jerkin. "You see, some time ago, I got candle wax on my favorite shirt."

Ambrosia's eyebrows raise as the prince pulls the jerkin over his head, followed by the shirt. I would glare at her, but my gaze also finds Henri's toned upper body, and I'm helpless to look away.

He must have been a formidable knight.

Oblivious to the effect his bare, muscular torso is having on the room, Henri offers Ambrosia his shirt. "If you can remove the wax—without using your magic—I will marry you."

The princess's eyes wander over Henri before she finally meets his eyes. "That's impossible. No one can wash away tallow wax."

"Sophia can," Henri says, glancing over and catching me staring. He suppresses a smile when my eyes fly to his. "Can't you, Sophie?"

Slowly, I nod.

"To the washroom." Amara leads us from Henri's chamber. We travel to the ground floor of the palace. When the queen opens the door, we're met with heat and steam.

"Go on," she snarls at Ambrosia, who looks rather put out to be asked to do something so common.

The laundry maids gape at us, most likely surprised to find the queen in their lair. Like Johan, they haven't bothered to enchant themselves. They're tall and perhaps a bit homely, but nothing how I envisioned trolls to look.

Ambrosia flounces in and stops in front of a vat of hot water. Holding the shirt between her thumb and finger as if it's poisoned, she dunks the fabric twice and then lets it drip.

"Hmmm," she says thoughtfully as she looks over her shoulder and flashes her mother a wicked look. "Looks like I failed."

Losing patience, the queen rips the shirt from her daughter and scrubs the wax with her own hands. The wax begins to spread in the garment, turning black.

"Soap!" Amara hollers at the troll girl closest to her. The poor laundry maid peeps in fright and hastens to find the queen a bar.

The queen scrubs and scrubs, growing angrier by the minute. The maids tremble by the walls, terrified they are going to take the brunt of the queen's anger.

"You can do it, can't you?" Henri whispers after thirty minutes have gone by.

Slowly, I nod and whisper back, "I think so, but it would have been easier before Her Royal Trollness got her hands on it."

Apparently having overheard me though I tried to be quiet, Ambrosia chokes back a laugh. It's enough to catch the queen's attention, and she whirls around to face us. Her hair is soggy, and her face is red from the steam. Her hands look scorched, yet the stain is still there.

One of the laundry maids lets out a small sound of distress, but the queen's eyes are firmly fixed on me.

"You think you can do better?" She stalks forward, and Henri's soaked shirt drips on the stone floor as she walks. Once she reaches me, she thrusts the soggy garment into my hands. "Be my guest."

Hoping it will work even when the fabric is saturated, I glance around the room, looking for an iron. There's one in the fire, already hot.

Here goes nothing.

"I need two pieces of scrap fabric," I say to one of the maids. "Anything you have will do."

Immediately, she fetches me a rabbit skin.

"Anything but *that*. I need cloth."

Several minutes later, I have the two pieces of fabric on either side of the wax stain, and I carefully lower the iron onto the cloth. The water hisses as it meets the hot metal. After several moments, I pull the iron back. To my relief, the wax is beginning to transfer to the scraps.

I repeat the process over and over, and once the wax is gone, I take it back to the hot water for a final scrub.

Five minutes later, Henri's shirt is as good as new.

"There," I hold the shirt out for Ambrosia to inspect.

The princess's face lights. "You actually did it! You are a clever human, aren't you?"

"You'd be amazed at what we've learned to do without magic," I deadpan.

Ambrosia laughs and hands the shirt to her mother. "Well, there you have it."

"No," Amara says, her face growing red again. She turns to Henri. "You tricked me!"

Henri shrugs. "You knew the terms. Why would I pick something I wasn't confident Sophie could do?"

With an inhuman shriek, Amara lunges forward. Before any of us can stop her, she sends her magic right at Henri. From the wild look on her face, I know she means his death.

"No!" I scream, but Ambrosia holds me back.

Just as the green magic hits Henri, a shield of purple flairs around him. We watch in horror and shock as the troll queen's magic ricochets right back at her. She screams again, this time in pain, and crumples to the ground.

The entire room goes deathly silent as we wait for the queen to move. Amara's cloaking magic is gone now, and her true form is revealed. She's gangly, and her joints are gnarled. Her hair is still thick, but it's coarse and no longer glossy.

It's a sobering sight.

After a full minute, a brave maid inches forward and places her hand on the queen's wrist, checking for a pulse. She purses her lips and turns to Ambrosia, her voice shaking with fear. "I'm sorry, Your Highness. The queen is dead."

CHAPTER 14

*A*mbrosia pats my head. "You would have made a lovely pet."

I roll my eyes at the new troll queen.

"Don't forget to prepare my gold," she reminds us.

We stand just outside the palace, in a snow-covered courtyard. It's frigid, but soon Henri and I will be back in Briadell. Where it's also frigid.

Oh well.

Ambrosia's taken the death of her mother better than expected. When the last of Henri's protective fairy magic sent the death curse back at Amara, I feared we'd have a war on our hands. Mortimer warned the results of the two magics mixing were unpredictable at best. I suppose he was right.

The princess has taken comfort in her mother's great collection of jewelry. She wears a crown of silver and rubies now, proclaiming that she's the new ruler of Elsland. Our kingdoms are officially allied, though I don't believe we'll be making any roads between the two anytime soon.

"You may come back and see me whenever I feel like it," Ambrosia says warmly, and *yes*, I'm sure she meant to say it exactly as she did.

Henri takes her hand and bows over it in respect. "I would say it was a pleasure, Your Majesty, but that would be a lie."

She grins. "And I could say I like you better with your shirt on, but that would be a lie as well."

Before Henri can answer, bright light surrounds us, and we're abruptly dropped onto the terrace outside Henri's palace.

Sitting there, on a chair smack-dab in the middle of the balcony, *knitting*, is the fairy from the village. Rynn's cat sits on her lap. The beast hisses the moment she spots me.

I almost feel bad for the scraggly cat. Here she thought she had this great big palace all to herself.

"I've come to return your cat," the fairy says as she looks up and smiles. "She's such a sweet creature. I must admit I'm going to miss having her around the cottage."

The beast lets out a low, angry yowl, leaps from the woman's lap, and runs down the stairs, toward the sad, snowy kitchen garden.

"Are you sure you don't want to keep her?" I ask the woman. "It seems the two of you have grown close. I hate to separate you now."

The fairy lets out a knowing laugh and stands. With a wave of her hand, her knitting and chair both disappear. "You did well, Sophie."

Henri narrows his eyes at the woman. "I know you. Why?"

Smiling, she cocks her head to the side, waiting for it to come to him.

"You're the first fairy the council sent," he finally says, narrowing his eyes. "What are you doing here now?"

"You don't really think I'd give up on you just because you told me to, do you?" she asks. "You've helped so many people in the village. It was our turn to help you. A handsome, chivalrous young man like yourself couldn't live under that awful, twisted curse indefinitely."

"And Mortimer?" I ask her.

"I suggested the council send him to Henri as punishment for—" She pauses. "That doesn't matter. I told him to find Henri a bride—someone who wouldn't run the moment she learned the prince was a bear. And look what a surprisingly good job he did."

She beams at us as she raises her hand, ready to wink out. "No need to thank me. Your happiness is more than enough."

And then she's gone.

I turn to Henri, not sure what to say.

A slow smile builds on his face. "Yes, look what a surprisingly good job he did."

Something has gnawed at my mind since the troll queen's death. It's time I get it out in the open.

"You're free now. You can have anyone."

He narrows his eyes. "You're my wife—and believe me when I say I can only handle one."

I almost laugh. "You know what I mean. Henri, you don't have to stay with me—"

Before I can finish, he pulls me into his arms. "Enough."

But I'm bad at taking orders. "I love you."

I gulp, terrified.

His eyes soften. "And I love you."

"Do you swear you wouldn't rather have someone else? Someone who's more genteel?"

"Do you swear you wouldn't rather have a man who didn't prowl the forest as a bear?"

I laugh and stand on my toes, closing some of the distance between us. My heart thrums with the memory of our last kiss.

Henri hovers his lips along mine, teasing, sweetly taunting—most likely purposely tormenting me for questioning his skill. It's delicious torture, and I close my eyes, trying to wait it out.

Drifting slowly, the prince grazes my temples and cheeks before he finally follows the line of my jaw back to the corner of my mouth.

"What happens now?" I ask, distracting myself.

He loops his arms around my waist, keeping me tucked close. "Now I take control of my kingdom, prepare a ridiculous amount of gold for the new ruler of Elsland, and crown you as my queen. It will be a horrible amount of excitement when all I want to do is spend my time with you."

"I'm not going anywhere." I brush my fingers through the hair at the base of his neck, pulling him just a bit closer. "And I happen to adore excitement."

"You don't say."

Surrounded by pristine, freshly-fallen snow, Henri

finally kisses me—and properly at that. The feel of his arms around me, holding me in the middle of the day, fills me with such happiness, I have no idea how I'll contain it all.

"Henri?" I ask after several minutes of basking in his new humanness.

"Hmmm?"

"Somewhere in our hectic schedule, do you think we could find time to visit my family? I'd like to show them you're no longer a bear." I pull back. "Or cursed...or the villain of children's nightmares."

His eyes crinkle with disbelief as he grins. "I think we can manage that."

He sets his forehead against mine, and he sighs. It's a sound of soft happiness, and it mimics the joy in my own heart.

It's hard to believe that it was only a few months ago I ran away from home in the middle of the night and Mortimer brought me to Briadell. Someday, I'll have to write Peter and tell him I did find adventure—one better than I could have imagined.

Startling me out of my reminiscing, Henri scoops me into his arms. I squeal in surprise as the no-longer-cursed prince carries me into the palace.

From above, a songbird sings from its perch on a turret, welcoming us home.

Entwined Tales **continues with Elisette's story, *A Beautiful Curse: A Retelling of The Frog Bride* by Kenley Davidson.**

Follow your heart and you could end up snacking on flies...

When a bumbling fairy godfather gifts a humble woodcutter's fourth child with extraordinary beauty, she spends the next eighteen years trying to hide it—behind a book. Now, Elisette is ready to follow her dreams and become a scholar, but her admirers keep getting in the way of her ambitions. Ellie knows better than to rely on her fairy godfather, but she's desperate enough to risk asking him for help. The trouble is, Mortimer isn't feeling very helpful. In fact, he's downright irritated...

After a bit of vengeful fairy magic, Ellie discovers that webbed feet and green skin are even harder to manage than beauty. No one cares what happens to a frog, except maybe quiet, unassuming Prince Cambren, who has enough troubles of his own.

Will Ellie find a way to break her curse and live happily ever after? Or will she spend the rest of her life eating flies and living in a pond at the back of the palace garden?

Everyone wishes they had a fairy godmother to make the world a little more magical...

They've never met Mortimer.

Every good deed merits a reward, at least according to the Fairy Council. But when a kind woodcutter's family is rewarded with a grumpy, sarcastic, irresponsible fairy godfather named Mortimer, their lives are changed forever… and not in a good way.

Follow the woodcutter's seven children as Corynn, Eva, Sophie, Elisette, Martin, Anneliese, and Penelope head out into the world to find adventure, new friends, and their very own happily-ever-afters. Their greatest challenge? Avoiding their fairy godfather's disastrous attempts to help.

Welcome to the Entwined Tales—six interconnected fairy tale retellings by authors KM Shea, Brittany Fichter, Shari L. Tapscott, Kenley Davidson, Aya Ling, and Melanie Cellier. Join the fun and enter the brand new world of the Entwined Tales for six enchanting stories filled with humor, magic, and romance. To sign up for the series newsletter to receive information about upcoming releases and more, visit ***www.entwinedtales.com****!*

A Goose Girl
K. M. Shea

An Unnatural Beanstalk
Brittany Fichter

A Bear's Bride
Shari L. Tapscott

A Beautiful Curse
Kenley Davidson

A Little Mermaid
Aya Ling

An Inconvenient Princess
Melanie Cellier

Turn the page for a preview of *The Marquise and Her Cat*, the first book in Shari L. Tapscott's *Fairy Tale Kingdoms* series.

THE MARQUISE AND HER CAT

CHAPTER ONE

The cat stares at me from his perch on the windowsill. His fluffy, golden tail twitches back and forth like a pendulum, and I squirm under his gaze. Even when I look away, his green eyes never leave me.

Sunlight shines through slits in the closed shutters, and dust motes dance in the air. It's daytime; he should be in the mill, catching mice. But, as if he knows Mildred's dying, he waits with us.

Before my eccentric aunt fell ill, she would talk to the cat—have real conversations with him. She'd even answer like he was actually speaking to her. It was the strangest thing. Disconcerting and unnatural.

My brothers, Thomas and Eugene, sit at the table with their hats clutched in their hands as we wait. The village doctor has been in Mildred's room all afternoon. When we woke this morning and found her barely breathing, we didn't expect her to make it past noon. It's nearing evening now.

The tiny cottage is too still. I'd like to open the shutters and let in the warm spring air, but the darkness feels right for the occasion.

Needing something to distract me from the cat's intense stare, I pick up my darning from the basket next to my chair. Eugene, the eldest of us, ripped his best shirt last week. Unlike the old brown rag he wears now, this one hasn't needed mending yet. Now it will match all the rest of ours.

My dress has so many patches, it looks like a quilt. With each of my growth spurts, I've added another layer to the hem and occasionally let out the waistline. At seventeen, I think I've finished growing. Maybe after the harvest we'll finally have enough money for me to buy material for a new one—if Mildred leaves the mill to us, that is. If she doesn't, I don't know what we'll do.

Mildred's door opens, and we all turn. The silence is palpable. The doctor nods. His expression is solemn, remorseful. I let out a held breath.

It's over.

Our aunt was a strange woman, and though I lived with her for ten years, I never knew her well. She kept to herself mostly, tending her garden and letting the boys run the mill. The only company she kept was that cat.

I glance at him now, morbidly curious to see if he will somehow sense her passing. Perhaps he'll mourn her loss —maybe he'll recognize the gloom weighing on my shoulders and wish to comfort me as well.

As I watch, the cat stretches. After arching his back and bowing low as if stiff from his morning in the sill, he stands on his hind legs and lifts the window latch with his nose. Without so much as a backward glance, he presses the shutters open and jumps outside.

He's a very odd cat indeed.

∼

"To Eugene, Mildred has left the mill and cottage," the ancient village clerk tells us.

My brothers and I sit in front of the man's desk, pretending our entire livelihood doesn't depend on what he's going to tell us. When he says the words, we all visibly relax. Though we hadn't discussed it out loud, each of us worried Mildred had sold the deed back to the baron at some point in the last few years.

The man owns most of the village, and his rent goes up every summer. With the meager amount our mill brings in, there's no way we could afford to stay.

The clerk continues, "And to Thomas, she has left the donkey."

I sigh, sitting back in my chair. There's nothing else. Should my eldest brother decide to take a wife, which he likely will if Sarah-Anne, the butcher's daughter he's been courting, has a say in the matter, there will be nowhere for me to go.

"To Suzette…"

I suck in a breath, surprised, and sit up straighter. What else did my aunt own?

"Mildred has left her cat."

From the corner of my eye, I see Eugene and Thomas share a startled look.

"I beg your pardon?" I ask, sitting unnaturally still.

The *cat*? That's just an insult.

The clerk frowns at the paper and adjusts his frames. He shakes his head and then pulls a tiny, jingling coin pouch from his desk drawer.

My heart leaps. There might not be much there, but it's at least something.

"And this"—he holds the money between us—"goes to Master Puss."

This time, I look at my brothers. "Who is Master Puss?"

The clerk clears his throat. "I believe it's the cat, Etta. And it says here that the money is to be used to buy him a pair of boots."

A lump forms in my throat. "Boots…for a cat?"

Looking uncomfortable, the clerk gives me a sympathetic nod.

I blink several times as I accept the pouch. Truly, Mildred was mad.

The clerk goes over a few more legalities with my brothers, but I'm too consumed with humiliation to listen. My aunt, my own flesh and blood, left the last of her earthly savings to a barn cat—for a pair of boots, no less. Boots for a cat when I haven't had a new dress since I was thirteen.

I rise when my brothers stand, dip when the clerk gives me a respectful nod, and follow Eugene and Thomas out the door. We startle a goose, who must have decided the entry was a good spot for her afternoon perch sometime while we were inside, and she squawks as she waddles several paces away, flapping her wings with indignation.

Oh, goose, I feel your pain.

Around us, the village bustles with activity. It's a market day, and farmers from the outskirts have hauled in their early spring crops. There are stalls with spinach, radishes, and all kinds of lettuce. The tailor's young son and daughter have even set up their own makeshift stall and are selling asparagus that they must have picked near the large creek that runs outside of town.

The vegetable grows with profusion this time of year. I can't see a reason to pay for it when I can gather it myself, but there are people more benevolent than I am. Or, rather, people with money to waste. How I'd love to have a few coppers in my apron pocket to give to the girl and boy. I'm sure they're hoping to make enough to visit the new chocolatier who's just opened his shop in the main square.

It's very fancy—a little too fancy for our quaint village, truth be told.

Still, I hope the young man does well. He wears finely-tailored coats and has a hat to match each pair of boots he owns. Though I would never admit it to Eugene or Thomas, I like to look at him. Like to imagine that someday he might look back.

"Etta, where's your mind?" Thomas laughs like I've done something humorous.

I jerk my head toward him. "What?"

He's a year older than I am, a year younger than Eugene, and he's as ornery as the donkey he inherited. And right now, he's grinning at me. "You just stepped in goose droppings."

I groan as I pull my skirt aside so I can examine the slipper. Disgusting greenish goo is smeared along the thin leather bottom. With one foot in the air, I stumble and then hop backward a few times to regain my balance.

Eugene's eyes go wide, and he holds out a hand. "Suzette—"

The warning is too late. I've already backed right into

someone. I leap forward and whirl around. "I'm so sorry…"

The words die on my lips, and I gulp. At first horrifying glance, I mistakenly think it's the young man from the chocolate shop, and I freeze in mortification.

But, no. This man is a stranger. His hair is corn silk blond, and his eyes are blue. But like the chocolatier, he wears a fine coat with well-cut breeches, and his boots are made of expensive leather. Along with a dagger, a rapier hangs from his baldric and rests at his hip.

With the way he's dressed, he must be a lord's son at the very least, perhaps even the offspring of a duke or an earl.

And, right now, his eyes are laughing at me.

My face flames, and for one brief moment I consider darting down the street to hide.

The young man bows. "Good day, mademoiselle."

Let me die right here on the street.

I dip in a curtsy and lower my eyes to the cobblestones as I mumble, "To you as well, monsieur."

I'm extremely conscious of my skirt with all its patches and my goose-dropping-smeared slipper. Never has such a fine man addressed me. Not once, not ever.

"Perhaps you can help me," he says. "I'm looking for the bookshop."

"It's just around the corner," Eugene offers, obviously embarrassed for me—or possibly of me. "The first building on the right."

The man looks at Eugene and nods his thanks, and then, just as he's about to step away, he hesitates. Turning to me, he says, "Do you think you could show me?"

"Me?" I blurt out before I can think better of it.

Eugene cringes and Thomas, trying to keep himself from laughing, bites his bottom lip so hard it turns white.

"Yes…yes, I'd love…of course," I stutter, feeling like even more of a fool than I did before.

Giving me a polite, refined sort of smile, the man offers me his arm. Practically trembling, I accept. He nods to my brothers, wishes them a good day, and leads me away.

ABOUT THE AUTHOR

Shari L. Tapscott writes young adult fantasy and humorous contemporary fiction. When she's not writing or reading, she enjoys gardening, making soap, and pretending she can sing. She loves white chocolate mochas, furry animals, spending time with her family, and characters who refuse to behave.

Tapscott lives in western Colorado with her husband, son, daughter, and two very spoiled Saint Bernards.

Sign up for Shari's fantasy newsletter and get a welcome letter with all kinds of book goodies, including several short stories and two novelettes!

Click here to subscribe

shariltapscott.com

Made in the USA
Monee, IL
12 June 2020